Heartwarming Horse Stories

Complied by Marsha Hubler

ISBN: **099719720X**
ISBN-13: **978-0997197204**

CONTENTS

FOREWORD

As a horse lover from day one, I've always had a passion to read about horses and to write about them. To date, I've published 16 books about horses or books that have a "horsie" presence in them.

However, in this special collection, instead of writing the tales myself, I recruited six other excellent authors to share their heartwarming stories about what I consider the most beautiful animal God ever created.

So kick off your boots, relax in your favorite chair, and enjoy these stories, sure to warm your horse-loving heart.

Compiler: Marsha Hubler
Best-selling author of
The Keystone Stables Series
www.marshahubler.com

The following story is a fictional account. Any resemblance of the characters to any persons, living or dead is purely coincidental. But this is a fictional account with a frightening potential to become reality in far too many riding stables across the country. Drug misuse and overuse in parts of the horse industry are rampant and so common most people don't even recognize how abusive the practices are to the animals and how potentially dangerous the abuse is to people trying to learn how to ride and handle horses. The time is NOW for responsible persons in the equine industry and the veterinary professional community, the vast majority of people involved with horses, to acknowledge the situation and DO something about it for the sake of all caring and conscientious trainers, riders and owners, and especially the horses.

Vanessa's W.R.A.T.H.

Lise Lund, VMD

You could have heard a pin drop as the little girl in her wheelchair slowly rolled into the courtroom. The attorneys watched the gallery and the jury; almost everyone in the room had eyes clearly welling with tears. The defendants and their counsel knew they were done, and they would lose, big.

Ten-year-old Vanessa had been fascinated with horses almost since she could first talk. She had begged for riding lessons since her sixth birthday. Her enchantment with the horse world escalated ten-fold when two of her best friends started lessons two summers ago. Vanessa's campaign intensified unmercifully from that time on. Finally when Vanessa turned nine, her mother relented and agreed to sign her up at a Hunter barn in the area. Mrs. James did so despite protests from Vanessa's father, struggling to convince herself along with him it would be okay.

The idea of her daughter riding had always scared Mrs. James. She had no interest in horses and neither did Vanessa's dad. They both considered the activity somewhat archaic and more than a little dangerous. When Vanessa had first started asking about lessons, her mother had surprised herself with how swiftly and firmly she said "No." Vanessa was their only child—a miracle born late in their married life after years of trying.

Vanessa had that wonderful, joyful optimism about life that comes from having always known she was truly loved by intelligent and caring parents. She had wanted for very little, but she wasn't spoiled. When love, time, and attention were what she needed, that was what she got, not an excess of material things, money, or organized activities. Vanessa's desire to ride caused Mrs. James quite a bit of internal conflict because Vanessa so rarely specifically asked for something for herself. Her parents enjoyed providing her with the opportunity to explore a broad array of endeavors. From there they almost always enabled her to focus intently on subjects that captivated her. They hoped this approach created a stimulating and fulfilling life for their daughter. Usually they anticipated her desires so well, she had little need to ask for anything. Mrs. James also knew her daughter was aware the expense of riding was easily within their means, so that wasn't the reason for denying this one special interest. And now these friends of hers had started lessons nearby....

In the midst of this development, Vanessa hadn't even whined or nagged. Her mother couldn't even scold her for a bad attitude. The little girl simply asked, very politely and nicely; she did it more frequently once her friends had started to ride, but always politely and nicely. It all but tortured Mrs. James to have to continuously say "No" and watch that joyful optimism be crushed once again.

When Vanessa related Jodi's and Sara's tales from lessons and shows, naming and describing their favorite horses, and even detailing all of them, laughing about the day Sara fell off the first time, Mrs. James began to re-examine her reasons for denying her daughter this "world" she somehow loved already, even if she'd only ever been there in fantasy and imagination. Mom knew the image of actor Christopher Reeve, in his wheelchair, had been a powerful influence in her mind. She'd been an ardent fan. He had been paralyzed in his riding accident on Vanessa's birthday, of all things. That image had come swiftly to her mind the first time Vanessa had asked to ride. It was what had made her "NO!" harsh enough to startle, and maybe even frighten Vanessa a bit. Mrs. James also recognized this was a little extreme and possibly quite unfair to Vanessa. If she was never going to allow her child to do anything potentially dangerous, then she should never be allowed to ride a bike, or drive a car, or date a boy.... She knew she was being overprotective, and, in the long run, it was a mother's attempt to keep her daughter safe by not letting her grow up. Her husband had agreed with that principle but still balked somewhat more strongly at the particular activity. His only knowledge of horses came from the stories his mother had told of her cousin Jake who trained racehorses. The general gist in all of them implied Jake basically amounted to a loser whether his horses won or not; and there were a lot of drugs and slimy behavior in the whole business. Mr. James didn't want his daughter whom he loved so dearly involved in such inequity.

Mrs. James had argued that was racing. Vanessa just wanted riding lessons. The breaking point had really come when she decided to take Vanessa to the stable one day while Jodi and Sara were having their lessons so Vanessa could watch. Mrs. James knew she was lying to herself when she thought this might appease her daughter's interest a bit. While there, she made it a point to chat with Jodi's mom and Sara's dad.

Jodi's mom talked about how the owner and head trainer, Mrs. Chase, taught with such total passion and drive, everyone excelled. "The woman has been at this a long time and really knows her stuff. And she has a wonderful junior trainer, Diane, who just loves teaching the younger kids." Jodi's mom went on to explain that sometimes Mrs. Chase could get impatient with beginners, so she handed them off to Diane, who had started out wanting to be an elementary school teacher but had found an even more fulfilling niche teaching beginner riding instead.

Sara's dad, a doctor, bragged about the stable's proven

success, pointing to the wall full of trophies and ribbons. He emphasized, "Sara's been winning ever since she first started showing with this barn."

But what ultimately convinced Mrs. James that she should allow her daughter to start taking horseback riding lessons was simply the look on Vanessa's face every time she touched one of the horses, the way she obviously rode every stride as she watched Jodi come down a line of fences, and, the clincher, Vanessa's complete joy from being allowed to sit on Sara's school horse and be led a few steps (compliments of Sara's pushy dad when Sara's lesson was over). Mrs. James' normally fairly quiet and reserved little girl chattered with excitement all the way home, thanking her mother over and over for taking her "to watch." Mrs. James marveled at her child's gratitude and grace—or was it just shrewdness?—in that she never once asked for lessons for herself again in among the thank you's. The riding helmets, the controlled atmosphere, and the quiet horses— she had even petted one— all reassured Mrs. James.

A year of weekly lessons ensued. Vanessa couldn't get enough. Already a polite child, the then nine-year-old also never missed an opportunity to say "please" or "thank you" to her parents or to clean her room or do anything else asked of her, obediently, and with a bright attitude. And then in May there came the week her lesson day fell on her birthday, a special treat. Diane had been giving Vanessa most of her lessons. They were working toward Vanessa taking her first jump. Despite her enthusiasm, Vanessa had come along rather slowly as far as actual riding skills went. Mrs. James knew it was partly because her protectiveness had probably made her daughter a bit timid. However, in this situation Mrs. James felt fine because it made Diane take a special interest in her child.

Mrs. James had long since decided she preferred to have Diane teach her daughter. She found Mrs. Chase competent enough but objected to her military and demanding way of instructing. Mrs. James knew the owner was that way because that's what it took to make the kids win in the show ring, and winning was what made the whole place a success so....

But Vanessa didn't even seem to particularly care about showing, at least for now. She just loved being allowed to ride a horse. She loved being allowed to do anything around a horse; Mrs. James had to make her put the wheelbarrow, pitchfork, and shovel away more than once when it was past time to go home. And Vanessa loved Diane. It couldn't have been any better. Mom was even able to suppress the knot she felt in her stomach when Diane first started talking about Vanessa "taking that first jump" as an extra special birthday present. With Diane directing it, she knew it would be okay.

The momentous day arrived. Diane put Vanessa on Toby, a big, grey gelding. Vanessa had ridden him a few times before in preparation for starting to learn how to jump. Mom had listened to Vanessa talk about how Toby was a little more skittish than Suzy, the old, quiet mare she had had for all of her initial lessons. "But if you just pet his neck and talk to him a little bit, he's fine," she had told her mother more than once on the way home from the stables.

As the lesson began, Mrs. James saw Vanessa stroking away and all but chattering at Toby. She smiled and wondered just who was nervous on this special day. Toby seemed even quieter today than the other times Mrs. James had watched Vanessa ride him. She felt a tiny bit concerned about the look on Diane's face. She seemed more serious than usual.

Diane had Vanessa performing an exercise where the young rider made her mount trot over a series of equally spaced poles on the ground, a skill they had practiced frequently in previous lessons. The added challenge today required Vanessa to hold a "two point" or slightly standing position down the whole line instead of her doing the more usual "posting;" the latter is a rhythmic rising and sitting in time to the horse's trot, also a specialized riding skill, but a somewhat easier way to accommodate the forceful bounce created for the rider by that gait. Vanessa then learned to "crest release" at the end of the line, which meant she had to move her hands holding the reins farther up Toby's neck as they went over the last pole, simulating what would need to be done if the final pole on the ground were replaced by a true raised jump. Diane explained to Vanessa it was done so the horse could use his head and neck freely to make the jumping effort. If he felt tension on the reins as he started to lift up into the air he might fear the bit would bang him in the mouth. The young rider heard this loud and clear. She would absolutely do everything necessary to make sure she never hurt Toby or make him afraid.

Vanessa had done everything perfectly several times.

Toby, on the other hand, seemed a little bit clumsy today, banging some of the poles as he trotted over them. Diane weighed this against the fact that Vanessa was about to explode with anticipation because of the build-up she'd been given about the next part of today's lesson. The instructor had her student trot Toby down through a couple extra times because she didn't like him hitting the poles. He never did that. Diane thought a few more passes might wake the gelding up a bit. After Vanessa's fifth or sixth perfect effort, Diane knew she could delay no longer.

Other than the more serious look on the young instructor's face, Mrs. James had no extra concerns about the situation. She had seen Toby jump three-foot fences with other riders on him, so she was sure he'd take care of Vanessa. While Toby and Vanessa walked and rested for a few minutes, Diane set up a cross rail about eighteen inches high in the middle, replacing the last pole on the ground. It represented the tiniest and easiest of fences for a horse of Toby's talent, designed so Vanessa would get some help toward success from the obstacle itself. Just high enough so he couldn't trot over it, the "X" required him to not only make a legitimate jumping effort, but to also clear it in the best place, the center and low point.

Vanessa asked for the trot with a quick gentle squeeze from her legs on the grey's sides. She smiled confidently as she whispered something to Toby only he could hear. His ears flicked back to acknowledge her words, a little bit slower and a little bit droopier than the way he usually said "Got it!" to his pilot, Vanessa. The "droopy" move made her giggle momentarily as if he was trying to make her laugh so she could relax. She gladly accepted that relief as she focused on steadying their trot.

The determined but sensitive young rider gave Toby's neck one last gentle stroke with the fingertips of her inside hand as she made the turn to steer him down the line of poles. Her equitation remained perfect, heels down, knees softly secure in the jumping saddle's knee rolls with legs below quietly against the grey's sides. She would not waver or hesitate, even if "the jump" at the end of the line this time looked enormous to the girl. The title theme from a song, "Simply the Best," played in her head.

Toby again clunked the first pole but skimmed cleanly over the next three to the cross rail.

Then it happened. Vanessa reached a little more forward

in her crest release just as she was supposed to, and she made the clicking noise Diane had instructed her to make to encourage her mount. But instead of sighting the jump and gathering himself for the effort, Toby bulled forward "in trot" and seemed to only notice the last element had changed when he was nearly on top of it. He made a last-ditch, clumsy effort to fold his front legs, which weren't even together because he had forged all the way to the base of the fence in a mindless, plodding trot. It was too late. His leading leg failed to clear anything and slammed into the one pole. His other front leg didn't get that far. Instead of Toby folding it and rising over the jump, the leverage of the pole he hit with his first leg knocked his second one out from under him. He fell. Hard.

Vanessa, already in an extra forward position for the two point with a crest release, was launched like a torpedo over Toby as his head dropped toward the ground. She hit head first, the rest of her body snapping like a whiplash beyond where her helmet dug in on impact. She lay there at a very odd angle, not moving. Toby struggled and stumbled to his feet again, aware enough of Vanessa's motionless body to avoid stepping on it. He trotted off to the end of the ring, apparently unhurt.

"Vanessa!" Mrs. James didn't recognize her own voice when she shrieked and ran to her daughter's side.

Diane caught Toby at the far end, threw his reins to a barn hand and screamed, "Go call 911!" She ran sobbing toward the little girl and Mrs. James, only comforted the tiniest bit by the fact that she could tell Vanessa was still breathing, but that was about all.

Vanessa had broken her back. She would never walk again and would eventually only regain partial use of her arms.

*****

A couple weeks after the accident, even though Vanessa was still in intensive care, Mrs. James finally started going home at night instead of sleeping at the hospital. She and Mr. James had been holding their own on the guilt and blame end, trying to concentrate on Vanessa. About fifteen minutes after she returned one night around 9:30, Mrs. James heard a knock at the door.

She opened it to find an extremely distraught Diane, asking to come in, saying she had something very important to tell them. Mrs. James hadn't seen her since the first week after the accident. Diane had come to the hospital every day, sometimes waiting a few hours to receive permission to go into ICU for five minutes to see Vanessa. The first day had been a little awkward, but afterward, Mrs. James had let some of her massive concern for her daughter extend to this young woman as well. She had recognized all along Diane truly cared about Vanessa. She knew this tragedy tore at the young instructor deeply; her guilt, perhaps, exceeded Mrs. James' own. What Diane was about to tell them would leave the parents angry with even more anguish than they already were feeling. Mrs. James called her husband to the room, and Diane began.

Her voice, as well as her hands, shook as she said, "I know what this might make you think of me, but I can't live with myself any longer. There's something about Vanessa's accident you need to understand."

She then proceeded to describe a conversation between Mrs. Chase and herself, which had taken place the week before the accident and what had been done the day of the accident because of that conversation.

"I told her how well Vanessa had done at the previous week's lesson, and I thought she was finally ready to start going over fences." Looking at Mrs. James, Diane recounted, "I told Mrs. Chase you had mentioned the next week's lesson fell on Vanessa's birthday, so I thought the perfect present would be for her to start jumping that day."

Diane went on to say how she had been a bit disappointed in what she felt was Mrs. Chase's less than enthusiastic reaction to all this. "You know how she is, so stern and all business. I wish she had more patience with the ones who take a little longer. She gives me the students who need to work on their confidence and skills but never seems terribly pleased for them when they do start to make progress. She's always saying I baby the kids too much. Then she all but ignores me when I try to tell her they're working really hard and doing really well. Anyhow, I wasn't even sure she was listening, but as I started to go she asked, 'Who are you going to put her on?' When I said, 'Toby, she's ridden him before,' she said, 'Make sure you see me that morning then.'"

Diane started to cry. Vanessa's parents had no idea what "seeing Mrs. Chase that morning" meant. Mrs. James reached for both Diane's hands and gently asked, "Diane, what is it?"

"It meant she wanted me to drug him before Vanessa rode." Diane was sobbing now.

Mr. James became furious. Mrs. James just looked horrified, glancing between the two.

The truth came out. Diane was convinced Toby fell because of the tranquilizer Mrs. Chase had insisted he have for Vanessa's lesson. Diane had tried to dissuade her that day as well, noting Vanessa had ridden him without any before and they'd matched splendidly, performing brilliantly in those previous lessons.

Apparently the junior and senior instructor had disagreed on the pairing from the start. Mrs. Chase thought the gelding was too flighty for a beginner, especially one as timid as Vanessa. Diane felt just the opposite, knowing how much Vanessa loved the horses. She felt she could boost confidence for both horse and rider by making it Vanessa's job to pet him and talk to him as she rode. And as far as Diane was concerned, it had worked beautifully. Vanessa had completed four successful lessons on Toby. It had been an even bigger boost to Vanessa's limited confidence when Diane told her after the second one, "Most of the other girls need at least two years of lessons before they're ready to handle Toby." Vanessa had just beamed on hearing that.

Diane had been sure the big, sensitive gelding would respond well to the little girl precisely because her aids as a beginner were very quiet and light. As a rider Vanessa didn't demand anything, which meant she didn't intimidate the horse. In Toby's case, this meant he didn't get threatened and upset and start fighting his rider instead of just doing his job. Diane knew Toby knew how to do that just fine. She felt confident she could count on him to take care of Vanessa and get her around the ring safely because she knew such a nimble equine athlete would take care of himself well without the rider mandating it. Diane also knew Mrs. Chase didn't have the same opinion of Toby. She had observed it was probably because Mrs. Chase was such a strong rider. Every time the head trainer got on the grey they ended up fighting with Toby in a fit by the time it was over, whereupon Mrs. Chase would get doubly annoyed with him because she knew she couldn't get as good a ride out of him as many of the students could. Then sometimes, the drugs would come out, and Mrs. Chase would go at him again…to prove she could win.

The morning of the accident, Diane had been handed

three syringes and told to administer the drugs to Toby and two other horses a half hour before their scheduled lesson times. Diane tried her best to say something to Mrs. Chase: "I really don't think Toby needs—"

"I don't care what you think!" On this particular day, Mrs. Chase was more vicious than usual.

Diane had long ago gotten used to the two Mrs. Chases, the smiling and politically correct one who dealt with the wealthy clients and the other one—the marginally abusive one who gave orders to the staff. Diane had made up her mind to tolerate the latter because she did want to be a part of the Hunter horse world, and Mrs. Chase held the reputation of being the best around here. Diane knew she could learn a lot.

"You are the junior trainer here; remember that." Mrs. Chase all but snarled at Diane. "Mrs. James will have a cow if anything happens to her precious Vanessa. You should have cleared it with me before you ever let that kid ride Toby."

Mrs. Chase ruled with an iron fist. It was her way or the highway. Diane had been there five years, longer than Mrs. Chase had ever kept a junior trainer. Diane had noticed, increasingly in recent years, every time she tried to make an independent decision not in total agreement with Mrs. Chase, she got shot down, even if what she did proved successful. Indeed, Vanessa readily mastering Toby was probably the most blatant example of the scenario. Mrs. Chase didn't want to teach the child because she was shy (and might cry). Mrs. Chase also didn't get along very well with Vanessa's mother, whose main concern was the child's safety and enjoyment. Mrs. James couldn't have cared less about her daughter showing or winning. So it all but galled Mrs. Chase when Diane could put the same kid on a horse that usually gave the owner difficulty, and the child consistently had beautiful rides.

Diane had also noticed, increasingly in recent years, the "solution" to their disagreements was to give some kind of medication, usually tranquilizer, to the horse they disagreed on. In days gone by, it might have been resolved by Mrs. Chase getting on and doing some additional schooling with the horse or having Diane ride the horse while Mrs. Chase taught her what to do to further the horse's training. But lately, it was almost always, "Here, give him this," handing Diane a syringe. Diane had thought briefly about how it paralleled Mrs. Chase's increasing tendency to reach for a drink whenever things got stressful.

Diane had been a bit surprised when she'd gone to work at how often the horses were given medications. Mrs. Chase had said, "This is a business. I can't afford to have a bunch of horses standing around that aren't earning their keep giving lessons." Diane had been even more surprised when she saw how Mrs. Chase's veterinarian catered to her, doing whatever procedures she ordered such as injecting hocks and handing her any drugs she claimed she needed. The vet never seemed to do much of an exam, always taking for granted Mrs. Chase's prior diagnosis of the problem. He never asked why she needed tranquilizer, and he never felt it necessary to give any instructions or prescription for its use.

Diane had even tried to question the vet about it one day. She'd seen Mrs. Chase give a lame horse a low dose of tranquilizer because it acted as a pain killer so she could use him for a lesson. A couple hours later Diane checked the horse and, of course, he showed even more lameness than he had before the lesson. Diane wondered why the horse wasn't given "bute" (phenylbutazone) or something else to alleviate his pain all the time, not just during the lesson. When she questioned whether this was abuse, the vet simply said not to worry about it, Mrs. Chase was very experienced, and she knew what she was doing.

Although she would come to disagree even more strongly with Mrs. Chase about giving tranquilizer to horses that weren't lame to calm them for a lesson, after this conversation with the veterinarian, Diane ceased to question when the head trainer ordered an injection, accepting it as "business as usual," no matter what she thought. Diane's experience of having ridden one or two horses when they were drugged stood in conflict with what she was being told by these "professional and experienced" people. She didn't think it was fair or smart to ask the horses to do something athletic, especially something as demanding as jumping, when they were unable to respond with the normal quickness discipline required. They rode so "dull," Diane felt very unsafe as the rider. Maybe Mrs. Chase was a strong enough rider to get the horses to respond correctly when they were, in fact, being made slower and more uncoordinated by the drugs, but Diane didn't feel at all comfortable on a horse that felt "lazy." She preferred to take her chances riding out any high spiritedness—after all…wasn't that part of what "training" was all about?

Mrs. Chase insisted giving tranquilizer to the high-spirited ones made them safer. She did it all the time with some of the school horses she routinely used. Diane preferred to just use horses like Suzy, older, solid, and reliable. She also knew such horses were worth their weight in gold because they were not easy to find. You couldn't train just any horse to be a lesson horse. Mrs. Chase had sold some of the ones that didn't have the steady disposition required to carry multiple beginner riders every week to people who still boarded the horses with her. Those people usually only rode about twice a month. They would call ahead and tell Mrs. Chase they were coming to the barn so she could go ahead and give "the cocktail," as she called it, so the horse would be safe to ride when they got there.

It was a sad end point for the horse's "training" and an equally sad loss for the new novice owner. Those owners would never truly learn how to ride much less ever experience the many joys of true communication in developing trust with their mount. These wannabe riders who would never "be" also took Mrs. Chase's word a little too readily that the repeated doses of tranquilizer didn't harm the horse and should be used to make the horse easier to ride. It would have made a lot more sense (and would have cost a lot less money) if they'd just gone out and bought a motorcycle or a four-wheeler ATV to ride instead of a horse.

Early on, when Mrs. Chase first started handing the syringes to Diane to administer the drugs before Diane had ever ridden a horse after it had been given tranquilizer, the young trainer had been almost pleased she was being trusted with this "important" duty of "making the horses safer." Ever since her own rides on a drugged mount, she had done it in a perfunctory manner because Mrs. Chase had made it her job. But then came the morning with Toby. The guilt she needed to express to Mr. and Mrs. James was amplified by the fact that she, Diane, had given Toby the drug. Although Mrs. Chase ordered it, Diane had actually injected it. And she knew, just from the way he had fallen, it wasn't "just an accident." She had almost thrown the syringe away but had been afraid of something happening with Toby being too high without drugs—and that scenario would've been her fault. She also almost stopped the lesson when he kept hitting poles—he never did that when Vanessa or anyone else rode him without any tranquilizer. But stopping the lesson would have crushed Vanessa; she had never tried harder nor ridden better than she had that day. If only….

Even after hearing these dreadful extra details, Mrs. James didn't blame Diane. Before Diane's visit she had been avoiding blaming herself or anyone else by praying. She coped with her anguish, deep in thought. *My job,* she told herself over and over, *is to deal with cruel fate and do my best to help Vanessa do the same. She could have died. She's still here and needs my faith and love right now, not my fear and negative emotions.* But this new information did infuriate her. She was almost as angry about what had been done to Diane in the whole situation as she was for herself and Vanessa. Once she had the chance to think about it for a while, she knew she had missed some clues and ignored others. She knew she didn't like Mrs. Chase, but she had been persuaded by all the other parents telling her this was the best riding facility, by how well run things appeared to be. Worse, she remembered more than once, Sara's dad, the doctor, saying things like, "Sara's horse was a little high at the show, but

Mrs. Chase took care of it. She gave him something." He said it like it was still more evidence of Mrs. Chase's consummate skill as a trainer, as if drugging horses was a normal and necessary part of training and showing horses. Even with her limited experience in the horse world thus far, Mrs. James knew it wasn't true.

Mr. James went in a different direction. He wanted justice. He automatically assumed what had been done was illegal. He immediately wanted the responsible parties punished. His wife had concerns that Diane would be harmed since she actually gave the drug to Toby. Diane said she didn't care; she felt like she'd welcome punishment if it would ease the guilt of seeing Vanessa in the hospital bed and wheelchair. Vanessa's father didn't hold Diane ultimately responsible for crippling his little girl either. He promised Diane he'd do everything he could to make sure she was held blameless as long as she promised to testify about what was going on all the time at the stable.

What Mr. James found out as he tried to pursue justice infuriated him even further. He started with the local police, who told him there were no laws against people giving drugs to their animals unless the drugs in their possession were illegal. Horse tranquilizer was a legal veterinary drug. The only laws the police knew of addressing the issue of having legal veterinary drugs on personal property that still restricted giving them to animals had to do with food animals because the drug residue could be left in the meat and harm someone who ate it.

"But you have to get the Department of Agriculture and maybe the FDA to investigate it," they told him. "We can't." They understood his anger and frustration but told him there really were no state or even federal criminal drug laws that addressed what had been done to his daughter and his family by way of someone misusing drugs. The police did suggest, however, since these were prescription veterinary drugs that had been given, Mr. James should perhaps file a complaint with the State Board of Veterinary Medicine. He did so, naming Mrs. Chase and her veterinarian in the complaint.

Months passed until an investigator contacted Mr. James. She listened to the story with great sympathy. When Mr. James finished, however, the investigator freely admitted to him, "I really don't know anything about horses, riding, or most of veterinary medicine, for that matter, so I don't really know if this Mrs. Chase did anything wrong when she gave her horse that shot. I do know the Board won't do anything about her practicing veterinary medicine on her own animals unless maybe if she did surgery on one of them or something like that. They won't do anything about someone giving their horse a shot. It goes on all the time."

Mr. James fumed, "This wasn't 'a shot' like it was a vaccine or even some antibiotic meant to treat the horse because it was sick. This was a drug that made him clumsy and uncoordinated. And how can you not know anything about veterinary medicine when you're investigating a complaint to the Board of Veterinary Medicine?"

The investigator ignored his first statements and matter-of-factly and somewhat air-headedly answered his question. "There's a state law requiring complaints to the Board of Veterinary Medicine be investigated by people who have nothing to do with veterinary medicine."

Mr. James gritted his teeth. "That's the most idiotic law I've ever heard of. How can you determine whether or not someone's done something wrong when you don't even understand the difference between vaccines and tranquilizers?" His anger and disgust were escalating with what he now knew was just more patronization and a further waste of his time by a legal system that had its head in the sand about this entire issue.

The investigator then emphasized again, "This Mrs. Chase is legally allowed to give legal veterinary drugs to her animals pretty much any way she wants, although, technically, since this was a prescription drug, she should have been giving it according to her veterinarian's directions since he's the one who's licensed to practice veterinary medicine."

Mr. James said he had checked with several veterinarians who were willing to testify in court that giving tranquilizer to a horse and then allowing someone to ride the horse was not "practicing veterinary medicine" because no vet in their right mind would prescribe tranquilizer to be used for that purpose.

He then asked, "Doesn't that mean Mrs. Chase wasn't 'practicing veterinary medicine' when she drugged Toby? Doesn't this mean she did do something wrong?" Mr. James had very carefully worded the complaint, to protect Diane, to imply Mrs. Chase had given the drugs herself. He wasn't even sure if Diane giving the drugs might also be "legal" because she was Mrs. Chase's agent in the situation. "Agent" in the horse world, he had discovered, meant any person designated as such could legally do anything the owner could do as if they were the owner. He also knew full well Mrs. Chase, to protect herself, routinely forced Diane to give the drugs. Then Mrs. Chase had a scapegoat to blame in case something happened. She made sure she could always claim "she hadn't given the horse anything."

The investigator again gave half an answer to Mr. James' queries. "If Mrs. Chase wasn't "practicing veterinary medicine," then the complaint doesn't come under the jurisdiction of the Department because "practicing without a license" is what I'm investigating in conjunction with this complaint. Your complaint doesn't suggest any other kind of infraction," she smugly concluded with a bubble-headed smile as if he should be impressed with her legal comprehension of the Practice Act.

At this further utterly ludicrous escape from responsibility by the legal system, Mr. James blew up: "So vets with training can be punished, but there's no law in this state protecting my little girl from having her back broken, compliments of some unlicensed idiot pumping prescription drugs into a horse and then telling my wife it's safe for our daughter to ride the animal?"

The investigator indicated, indeed, there wasn't any law providing that kind of protection, at least not under the Practice Act.

"What about the loser-creep of a vet who kept supplying her with the stuff?" Mr. James asked. "I have witnesses who'll testify all Chase had to do was tell him what she wanted, and he handed her whole bottles."

The investigator explained, "The vet was allowed to do it because he had been to the farm and had what is referred to as a valid Veterinary Client Patient Relationship. It's all that's required for him to sell her legal veterinary drugs." She then asked if Mr. James had any more questions or statements.

"No," Mr. James barked and slammed the door as the investigator left.

About two months later, Mr. James received an official letter from the Bureau of Professional and Occupational Affairs, a part of the Department of State and the government division that oversees all professional licensees, including veterinarians. It said they had found no evidence of anyone acting in violation of the Practice Act and the laws governing the practice of veterinary medicine in the State under his complaint, so the case had been closed. Mr. James crumpled the letter and threw it in the trash.

Mrs. James and Diane went down a different road, trying to do something useful and positive with the energy coming out of their anger and guilt from the whole awful experience. They remained friends and became strong allies because Mrs. James recognized Diane genuinely loved Vanessa, plus she was a competent and intelligent trainer. She used her skillful understanding of both the horses and her students to absolutely minimize the inherent risk that's part of riding. She never lazily pretended this could be accomplished much more easily by way of misusing pharmaceuticals.

Mrs. James knew Diane's continuing to visit Vanessa provided an opportunity for both of them to heal and grow stronger. Beyond that, Diane's astute training had nurtured an unseen but vital part of Vanessa through the horses. She'd recognized Vanessa's naturally kind and caring, if somewhat timid, nature. She saw it as inextricably linked to the power of her tremendous motivation and enthusiasm for horses and riding. This wise young woman knew she could let horses help this special student develop the combination into a mature confidence with an underlying gracious self-discipline, which would permeate and benefit her whole life. Vanessa needed all of that part of herself intact and growing to use in a different way now in order to live boldly and well, despite the physical challenges she faced. Mrs. James had noticed during their visits that Diane could still find and inspire that part of Vanessa even on Vanessa's "down" days, even on days when Mrs. James herself could offer little consolation and encouragement.

The same day Diane had told Mrs. Chase she quit (and told her more than a few other things as well), Diane had registered to take the remaining courses she needed to complete her teaching certificate. She found a position at Vanessa's middle school. She also tutored Vanessa at home when necessary as a personal private duty, and she learned how to be an assistant caretaker to Vanessa.

In addition to caring for Vanessa, Mrs. James launched a personal crusade. With Diane's help, Mrs. James modeled her mission after M.A.D.D.—Mothers Against Drunk

Driving. They all had a good laugh when they decided to call the new organization "M.A.T.H.—Mothers Against Tranquilized Horses." During some of the tutoring sessions, Vanessa struggled with math assignments just as the two adult women always had when they were in school. Diane and Mrs. James appreciated the humor and irony of any women's group with "MATH" as its title. They figured it might afford their effort a little extra attention.

Mrs. James felt a kinship with the M.A.D.D. group in that she wanted something done about unknowledgeable and/or lazy, greedy people irresponsibly mixing drugs and riding. She wanted tougher laws. Indeed, knowing what her husband had learned, she wanted a law to address the issue as a crime since that's what it was. She reasoned driving cars obviously had a concerning level of potential danger from "true" accidents just as riding did, but M.A.D.D. was right in their outrage that some people constantly escalated the danger and often harmed or even killed innocent victims because they rationalized their drinking and driving, and it wasn't anybody's business but their own. Barn owners drugging horses they then had people pay to ride should be assigned the same kind of liability for their actions and the drugs' net effects.

Watching Diane and Vanessa over the preceding year, however, Mrs. James had also gained a huge appreciation for all the good that could come out of letting young girls work with horses. She knew perfectly well horseback riding wasn't going to go away any more than driving was. She felt her M.A.T.H. group had the right idea to demand some tough laws be instituted to punish the irresponsible, illicit use of drugs in a way that negated many of the fundamentally positive aspects of the activity while it introduced untold risk. M.A.T.H. wanted the message that substituting tranquilizer for training was nothing less than animal abuse while this completely improper utilization of pharmaceuticals was at the same time potentially devastating (or even deadly) for anyone participating in horseback riding, particularly if they were naïve about what was being done.

Mrs. James and Diane also decided to carefully explain the extra circumstances of the accident to Vanessa. Diane had rightfully pointed out Vanessa was better off knowing she had done everything right that day, and nothing about the fall had been her fault. The ten-year-old was happy to know Mrs. Chase had no reason to blame her for anything.

Vanessa knew full well Mrs. Chase had written her off as a nothing rider, never acknowledging her having ridden Toby quite successfully several times before the accident. One of Vanessa's first questions when she had revived after her fall was whether Toby had been hurt.

Mrs. James remembered marveling at her daughter's character in that crucial moment. She felt the same love and pride again during this conversation. Vanessa was far less interested in hating Mrs. Chase for what had happened to her than she was in being angry at Mrs. Chase for putting Toby at risk and apparently hurting other horses by the way she did things. Diane and Mrs. James thought it okay for Vanessa to hang on to the anger and use it to represent M.A.T.H. on behalf of the horses, as well as herself.

With Diane's influence, M.A.T.H. focused on getting the word out to youngsters that "training" a horse was not accomplished by giving a horse an injection—ever. The organization encouraged young people to report any form of abuse they saw, especially drugging, because it is a despicable substitute for true and careful training. They started a campaign within the veterinary colleges to make sure it was always emphasized to veterinarians in training that NO tranquilizers are to be used while a horse is ridden. They also created a partial course syllabus explaining how to use other therapeutic prescription veterinary pharmaceuticals appropriately in working horses, emphasizing how the drugs are just part of overall management systems designed to insure safety and soundness in these animals. Amazingly, it was the first course material of its kind at most of the universities, clearly teaching where to draw the line between the veterinarian's knowledge and training and that of professional horse trainers.

Not too long after Vanessa's accident, a group of other local riders became incensed when they learned Vanessa's story. Out of deep concern for the horses and children, the riders formed "W.R.A.T.H.—Women Riders Against Tranquilized Horses" in Vanessa's honor. They took the position that too many people like Mrs. Chase, who were either lazy, scared, or not skilled enough to train a horse properly (sometimes all three), and who were primarily interested in making money from horses as easily as possible, put an ugly image and a black eye on everyone else who was involved with horses. And they were tired of it. They were all as passionate about equines as anyone could be—essentially grown-up versions of Vanessa, who had experienced great pleasure and peace throughout their lives, compliments of riding, caring for and caring about horses. They didn't like being identified with people who abused horses and put naïve riders at risk on a regular basis. They began to lobby the state government, the Veterinary Board, and professional organizations to clean up the irresponsible distribution of specific veterinary drugs that had such potentially devastating consequences.

In the long run, Mr. and Mrs. James felt frustrated and infuriated by the minimal to non-existent laws and regulations overseeing the entire situation. They had never been a couple who thought lawsuits were a way to solve anything. However, they couldn't sit by while Mrs. Chase's liability policy insurance company offered them an enormous settlement, provided they kept the circumstances of the accident "quiet" and would say nothing about the State working on a liability law for the equine industry— a similar law had already passed in a majority of other states—that would make people like Mrs. Chase even less accountable for their actions.

Feeling they had no choice, Mr. and Mrs. James decided to sue. They wanted to make a point of Vanessa's case, and, as she reminded them, they also did it in Toby's honor. They brought suit against Mrs. Chase, her veterinarian, and even the distributor and the manufacturer of the tranquilizer:

You could have heard a pin drop as the little girl's wheelchair slowly rolled into the courtroom....

All the Pretty Little Ponies

Murray Pura

Dedicated to Jacinda Gore, angel horse girl

Jay loved to watch the wild horses run.

It was one of the few things she still enjoyed.

Her father would take the old Chevy pickup and go off the main road and follow washed-out paths for miles to get her to the valley the Mustangs loved. Sometimes they were there, sometimes they weren't. But when they were grazing in the valley, the sight filled Jay with light. The feeling made her imagine there was a sun inside her chest, and it was shining over everything.

"Thanks for taking me all this way, Dad," she would say.

Her father would tilt the straw Stetson back on his head and smile. "It's not so much to do for my girl."

"It takes an hour, and most of the time you have to drive over rough country."

"Not a problem at all."

Sometimes the sun in her chest would be covered by a cloud. "I wish I could ride again."

"You will, Jay."

"The doctors say I won't."

"Baker and Flint are good men, but they're not God. They're saying what they say based on their experience in medicine. It's not based on their experience with the Almighty."

"The breaks are so bad. And the pain in my knees and hips won't ever go away."

"We'll see."

"It's going to be two years. I'll be fourteen soon. Nothing's going to change. You and Mom have prayed so much, the whole world ought to be healed by now."

"Sometimes things happen fast with the Lord, like a flash flood spilling over the banks of the creeks and rivers. Other times it happens slow and easy, so slow and easy it feels like you've been asking for help for a hundred years."

Jay felt the blood drain from her face. "And sometimes nothing changes at all, and you have to live with it. That's what Pastor Luke says. You can only ask God for strength and joy to overcome whatever's brought you down. Like when Paul prayed for God to remove the thorn in his flesh, and he was told no; God's grace had to be sufficient for him. He never got healed, but in his heart he got stronger."

Her father ran his hand back and forth over the steering wheel. "Maybe you'll get both. A stronger spirit and stronger legs."

"Hasn't happened yet."

Samantha had thrown her, the family's wonderful palomino mare, not out of nastiness, but because of a rattlesnake. Jay had landed on boulders. No one had found her for two hours. There were broken bones in her hips, her pelvis, and her legs. Some bones had mended quickly and solidly; Dr. Flint had once said she was well on her way to full recovery. But other bones had not done so well, and Dr. Baker had told Jay she might not walk again without crutches, and riding would be out of the question. So she could watch the horses graze on her ranch, and she could watch them run free in the hills, but she could never saddle up a horse again...and gallop...and delight in the wind streaming through her scarlet and golden hair.

"Do you have a favorite Mustang out there?' her father asked one day.

The sun was firmly lodged in Jay's chest when he asked.

She grinned. "I like them all." She pointed. "That dappled gray. That black. That bay. They're all wonderful."

"Did you notice the new mother over there?"

"Where?"

"She's by that rocky outcrop."

Jay stared. "You mean the palomino? Why do you call her a mother?"

"You can't see the foal right now. Keep your eyes open."

Jay waited, fidgeting in her seat.

Suddenly the foal appeared, cautiously stepping out from behind the mare.

Jay put her small hand over her mouth. "Oh. It's beautiful. I wish I knew if it were a colt or filly."

"I don't think we'll ever get that sorted out. Not until it's grown up."

Jay was fascinated by the foal's awkward steps, the dark

copper and gold of its coat, the cloud whiteness of its mane and tail. It took milk from its mother for several minutes. After that, it looked around itself at the other Mustangs. When another foal came over to nuzzle it, the palomino jumped and ran behind its mother again.

Jay laughed. "It's so timid. I hope it learns to stand up for itself."

In the days following, Bill Price drove his daughter out to see the Mustangs every second day instead of once or twice a week. Jay's eyes scanned the herd from behind the cracked windshield, always searching for the palomino mare and its foal. Some days she could not find it, and the sun in her chest would disappear, and a thick gloom would fill her in its place.

"I hope nothing bad has happened," she would say.

Her dad would shake his head. "There's lots of range they cover we can't get to by truck. I'm sure you'll spot them with the main herd another day."

Jay would wrestle with anxiety once they had returned to the ranch, an anxiety that never went away until her father drove her back to the valley the Mustangs preferred. If she caught a glimpse of the palomino mare and its foal, she was able to relax and smile. If she didn't, she would clench her fists, without seeming to be aware of it, and tension would keep the skin on her face tight.

"Breathe easy," her father would say. "They'll pop up eventually."

"What if they don't?"

"Just rest easy. Don't get worked up about something that hasn't even happened. Save it for your homeschooling."

Jay pouted. "Homeschooling would be just fine if it didn't include homework. Or math."

*****

For a year they drove back and forth, and Jay was rewarded with a sight of the two palomino Mustangs more often than not. Then her father took time off from his many ranch chores and took her to the valley every day for two weeks, when she was thrilled to see them every day. After two weeks of watching the pair for hours at a time, she and her father came to the same conclusion at the same time: the foal was not a foal any longer; it was a yearling.

"Now we can't be one hundred percent sure," her dad cautioned. "After all, we don't watch them twenty-four/seven, do we? I haven't seen it taking its mother's milk like it used to, but I haven't seen it cropping grass either."

"I'm sure I spotted it grazing."

"When was that?"

"The moment we arrived. I know you cut the engine, and we coasted to a stop, but I still think it heard us and stopped."

"Well, we'll see. First one who catches it snatching up a mouthful of spring grass wins a Jimmy Jim's burger and fries and shake."

"It's a deal."

They sat in the truck and fought to keep their eyes on the yearling—if it really was a yearling—as scores of horses milled about it and its mother. Two stallions started a fight at the edge of the herd, kicking up clouds of dust. The clash disturbed the other Mustangs and made the herd move away toward the south.

"Oh, now we'll never find out," complained Jay.

"Go easy," her father replied. "One of the stallions just ran off. The herd will settle down."

"But there's too much dust."

"It'll settle."

Jay located the foal first but didn't tell her dad. It was

standing beside its mother, looking around, still cautious, still long-legged and slim, but with more height and more muscle than it had carried even three months before. As the herd quieted with the end of the fight between the stallions, the foal seemed to dart its gaze around less and stop swinging its head. It nuzzled its mother, and Jay was sure it was going to take milk.

So you're still a suckling after all.

Suddenly it lowered its head and began to work away at a large clump of grass.

"There! There!" Jay lifted herself off the truck seat with one hand and pointed with the other. "It's eating! It's eating!"

"I can't see anything."

"Oh, come on, Dad, it's right there. Follow my finger."

"I see the mare."

"You just don't want to pay up with the burger and fries. Look!"

Finally Bill Price grinned. "There it is. I wonder how the grass tastes after a year of only milk?"

"I'm sure it tastes incredible. It's a yearling. And I win the burger and fries at Jimmy Jim's. But we still don't know if it's a filly or colt."

"Your chair's in the back. You can wheel on down and take a look."

"No, thanks. I don't like using the chair if I don't have to, and I doubt if its wheels can handle the stones and sand. Plus…who knows how many stallions are down there?"

"It'll take years before we figure out whether it's male or female unless it gets real close to the truck."

"Well, it's never going to get real close to the truck anytime soon."

"You ready for Jimmy Jim's?"

"Not yet. Can't we sit here for another hour? They're all so beautiful, and the sky is a perfect blue today."

Dad settled back in his seat. "I'm in no special hurry. Take all the time you like."

"You're always in a hurry on the ranch."

"But this isn't the ranch. It's time out with the charming Jay Price on the open range."

"I wish it were all open range. Reynolds on one side of this valley and Knight on the other and both of them grumpy old men."

"It's a good thing they have the valley between them

then," replied her father, "otherwise they'd likely start shooting at each other."

"They're always sour. Even in church. I wish Pastor Luke would give them both a kick in the pants. He's big enough."

Dad grunted. "John Wesley said sour godliness was the devil's religion."

"Well, that about suits those two. They're in the devil's back pocket if you ask me."

"Sh-h."

*****

Jay slept well that night, the usual aches and pains in her legs and hips not bothering her as much. In the morning she remembered she had a math quiz, and her stomach turned over, but at the same time she remembered the palomino foal, and that took away most of the nausea caused by the thought of the quiz. She lay in her bed, expecting her mother to open the door any minute to help her up, but soon it was well after seven, and her mother hadn't appeared. Truck doors suddenly slammed outside her open window and gravel popped under truck tires. She heard her father shout, "It's under Federal protection!" Her mother said something

Jay couldn't understand, and her dad responded to that, but by then he and the truck were much farther away.

Jay sat up in bed. "What is it?" she called. "What's going on?"

She heard her mother's voice. "I'll be upstairs in a minute."

"Where did Dad go? What's wrong?"

"I'll be right there."

In a few moments her mother opened the door to Jay's room, her eyes red and swollen and the bun in her hair unraveled.

"Mom, what is it?"

Her mother sat on the edge of Jay's bed. "How did you sleep?"

"I slept okay, Mom, but I'm not sleeping now. Where did Dad take off to in such a hurry?"

"He got word an incident had occurred out at the edge of our property. He took your brother with him."

"An incident? What does that mean? What sort of incident? Has someone been hurt?"

Her mother smoothed back strands of Jay's reddish gold hair that had fallen over her brown eyes. "A number of the

Mustangs have been shot. Your father got word the shooters used a helicopter to do it. The sheriff is out there now. Federal agents are coming in from the city."

"Someone killed the horses?"

"Not all of them."

"How many?"

"We don't know. Your father is going to find out."

Tears flowed quickly down Jay's cheeks. "Who would do that? The Mustangs don't bother anyone. They're on land set aside for them. They're not on other people's ranges."

Her mother didn't reply but put her arms around her daughter and let her cry. After about ten minutes Mom encouraged her daughter to get dressed, climb into her chair, and come downstairs. The stairs had been converted into a ramp Dad had put in place after Jay's accident.

Jay wheeled herself into the kitchen, realized she had no desire to eat or drink, and wheeled herself out a side door into the yard, banging the screen door open with her feet. There were no dust clouds on their long driveway so she settled down to wait, wishing she had Kleenex so she could blow her nose. Without her having to ask, her mother put a box in her lap.

Sorrels. Dapple grays. Bays. Chestnuts. Pintos. Buckskins. Roans. So beautiful. So deserving of life, Jay cried. *I pray they're not all gone. Please, God.*

Jay's father and Shane were gone three hours, but she didn't budge. She still refused to eat but sipped a cup of water. Finally dust streamed into the air, and a few minutes later the newer black Ram pickup pulled up in front of the ranch house. Shane got out first, his blue shirt stained with blood.

"How many?" As soon as she asked she started crying again. "How many, Shane?"

"Fifty or sixty."

"Oh, no, so many! Who would do that? Who would be so cruel?"

"Ranchers who figure Federal Land should be theirs. Those who claim the Mustangs jump the fence and eat the grass their beef cattle need. The kind who think they're above the law." Shane paused and took off his black Stetson. "I'm sorry, Jay. I know how much the herd meant to you. But there are plenty of them still alive. They're just scattered all over creation now. Hard to get a good count."

Dad climbed out of the Ram. "How are you doing, Jay?"

"Not good."

"Shane's right. They didn't get them all. You can thank God for that."

"Fifty or sixty is bad enough." Jay struggled to talk, her cheeks covered in wet and her nose running. "Who did it?"

"Federal agents have the chopper and the pilot. He landed at some out-of-the-way place, but hands from the Cross Bar Ranch spotted him. They don't have the shooters…apparently there were two. The pilots talked. It was either that or take the fall for everyone involved."

"What did the pilot say?"

"Jay, I don't want to get into it."

"He must have told them who did it."

Her father put his hands on his hips. "Reynolds. He claims Reynolds payrolled the whole operation. I don't know if the Feds will be able to prove it."

"I knew it! I hate him! I hate him! What business does he have going to church and singing hymns? I hope God sends him to hell!"

"Save your breath, Jay. We have more important things to deal with." Dad nodded at his son. "We'll use the old barn. It's clean and quiet."

"Yes, sir."

Jay watched her dad and brother walk to the back of the truck and heard the tailgate slam down. They grunted and struggled for a few moments and reappeared carrying a thick tarp between the two of them. She saw a small horse's head protruding as they walked as quickly as they could to the old red barn.

"Who is it?" asked Jay.

"The yearling," her father replied.

Jay wheeled after them. "How badly is it hurt?"

"He took a bullet."

"He?"

"The yearling's a colt, Jay."

They laid the colt in a stall filled with fresh hay a few days before. Jay wriggled out of the chair and crawled to the colt's side. He was lying on his right side, and his left eye looked at Jay in fear. She began to stroke his mane and neck slowly and gently.

"Where's his mother?"

She saw Shane and her father look at one another.

"Is she dead?" she asked.

"Yes," said her father.

"Do you think…do you think she suffered very much?"

"No. Where the bullets hit her she would have died instantly."

Tears dropped from Jay's face onto the colt. "Even with the dirt and blood in his mane, it's all so white, just like a snowfall." She glanced over his body. "I see the bullet hole there by his hindquarters. Is that the only one?"

"So far as we can tell."

"Did you tell Charlie?"

"Me and Shane and some of the boys from the Cross Bar rescued about twenty horses. Charlie had to put a few down because the wounds were so bad. He's working to save the others. Most of them are worse off than this colt. We'll have to wait our turn."

"The colt's trembling."

"Here." Shane took a horse blanket with a Navajo pattern down from a hook and spread it over the colt carefully. "Charlie called for help from the vets in the next county and from the city too. Some of them are already working with him. It won't be that long before Charlie or one of the others comes out to help us. Meanwhile, he told us we've got to try and reduce the shock. We've got to keep him warm and dry and feeling safe. I'll get a bucket of water, but I don't know if he'll lift his head enough to drink it."

"Is the bullet still in him?"

"Yeah."

Jay continued to stroke the colt's head and neck. She talked to it in a soft voice.

Her father dropped to one knee beside her. "I want him to make it."

"He will, Daddy."

"Charlie said he might have to put him down. He's so young, and he may have a broken leg."

"No, we can't!"

"Look, this isn't Hollywood, and we aren't horse whisperers. The colt's really suffering. We'll do our best for him 'til Charlie shows up. But if he has to euthanize him, that's the route we have to take. For the animal's sake."

"What about my sake?"

"There's plenty of other horses. Plenty of other palominos."

"There aren't plenty of other Mustangs we saw grow from a baby into a big strong boy right in front of our eyes."

"Sure there are."

"Not like him." The tears started again. "He's just like me now. Can't walk. Can't stand up. No future."

"Jay."

"We're both the same. You can see we're both the same. If you put him down you might as well put me down too."

"Don't talk crazy."

Dad tried to put his arm around his daughter, but she shrugged it off.

"We have to save him" she cried. "There's so much bad out there. We have to save him and show everyone the bad doesn't win out."

"Jay, he took a bullet from a high-powered rifle."

"I don't care. What good are all our prayers and medicines if we can't save one colt from a cold-blooded murderer like Jake Reynolds?"

"I'm sure there's hope." Jay's mother was standing at the open door to the barn. "We have a lifetime of prayers floating around the Price Ranch. There has to be enough strength in those to raise up a wounded colt."

They all looked at her, the late morning sunlight catching in her hair and dress.

"Thank you, Mom," said Jay.

The sound of a truck brought Dad to his feet.

A short, chubby man in suspenders and a battered cowboy hat came briskly into the barn, shaking Mom's hand and making his way with a bow-legged gait to the colt. He nodded to Dad and Shane, squeezed Jay's shoulder, and sat down by the back legs of the yearling.

"I'll need a basin and hot water, Mizz Char," he said in an accent Jay had heard came from Mississippi, "and a good number of towels."

"Yes, Charlie." Jay's mother left the barn quickly.

Charlie peeled back the horse blanket. "My other vets are still working hard. Now I'm giving this boy a shot for the pain and another for the infection. Then we'll get the bullet out. You going to assist, Jay?"

"Yes, sir."

He glanced at Jay. "We have some luck on our side. I can see by the entry wound we have a smaller bullet. One shooter had a 7 Rem Mag. I know because I use one myself for hunting. But the other shooter had an AR-15 with a much smaller bullet at 5.56 mm. Sure, still high velocity, but it didn't break any bones as far as I can see. We're gonna get it out, Jay, and you're going to help—all right?"

She nodded, wanting to hope, afraid to hope too much.

Charlie checked the colt's heart with his stethoscope, opened his bag, took out two vials and two syringes, pushed the needles of the syringes into one vial or the other, and gave the yearling both shots. The colt lifted its head and murmured, but when Jay continued to soothe him, he laid back down again.

Mom arrived with the basin and towels, Charlie pulled a small flashlight from his bag, asked Jay to shine it over the wound, and he began to probe for the bullet. The colt whimpered, and both Jay's parents knelt beside him and spoke to him.

"There." Charlie showed them a small bullet. "It wasn't in deep. Most of its force must have been spent. Perhaps it was a ricochet."

He washed around the wound with the water, dried it with a towel, and applied a square of gauze. He listened to the colt's heart again and returned the stethoscope to his bag. Then he stood. "I'll come by this evening to see how he is. There's bound to be a fever. His stifle, his hindquarters here, they're bound to be sore on the left side. But the medication should bring the pain and inflammation down.

We'll try and get him on his feet in a couple of days."

"Thanks, Charlie," Dad said, standing and shaking the vet's hand.

"No problem. I'll just get back and see how the others are getting along." He smiled at Jay. "I reckon you'll be sleeping beside your colt tonight."

"Yes, sir."

"Perhaps he'll sit up and drink for you. Do you have a name for him yet?"

"Snowfall. Because his mane and tail are so white."

"They are, aren't they? Keep your spirits up, Jay. I'm confident he'll pull through."

"Thank you, sir."

The only time Jay left the colt's side that afternoon was to use the washroom in the house. The rest of the time she stayed in the barn. It seemed to her the yearling was getting worse, but she didn't speak her thoughts out loud because she was afraid it would make the worst happen. Her father and brother did the ranch chores, and her mother brought her cheese melted on toast and a glass of milk, but no one mentioned the math quiz or her homework. The stars twinkled by the time Charlie came back.

"He's sleeping a lot," said Jay.

Charlie examined the wound and checked the horse's heart with his stethoscope. "Right now that's the best thing. I'll be back at dawn to check on him again," he said as he walked out of the barn.

Mom brought her daughter a pillow, a quilt, and a thermos of water. The colt still hadn't shown any interest in the water bucket by his head. He did open his left eye and gaze at her as she stroked his muzzle and sang a nursery rhyme to him she'd always liked:

"Hush a bye

Don't you cry;

Go to sleep my little baby,

When you wake

You shall have

All the pretty little ponies.

Paint and bay, sorrel, and gray

All the pretty little ponies.

Hush a bye

Don't you cry;

Go to sleep my little baby,

When you wake

You shall have

All the pretty little ponies,

All the pretty little ponies.

"Please live, Snowfall," she whispered. "Some days I don't feel like living. If you and all the Mustangs are gone, I'll give up altogether. I've got a lot of pain too, and my legs won't work. But if you stick around for me, I promise to stick around for you." She prayed and fell asleep with one arm around the colt's neck.

*****

The next morning, Charlie woke Jay when he squatted by the yearling and began to change the dressing on its wound.

"Did he drink?' Charlie asked as he finished with the gauze and took a rectal thermometer out of his bag.

"I don't think so."

"We have to get him hydrated. His temperature is dropping, so that's a good sign. I'll give him more injections for pain and inflammation, and maybe he'll get to the point where he's interested in water again." He looked at her as he used his stethoscope. "Strong heartbeat. How did you sleep, Jay?"

"It was all right."

"Warm enough?"

"Yes, sir."

"Here comes your mother with something hot. All right. I'll be back tonight. Try and coax him to drink."

"How are the other Mustangs?"

"We lost one more. But the rest are doing well. The herd still hasn't returned to the valley though. I expect the smell of blood and death will keep them away for a while."

"Good morning, Charlie." Mom walked in with a cup of hot chocolate for her daughter. "Can I persuade you to stay put long enough to enjoy some waffles and sausages and hash browns?"

"Normally you could tempt me," Charlie said. "But we need to see to those Mustangs. I'll stop by this evening."

"All right. Thank you."

Jay's mother handed her the cup. "Were you comfortable last night?"

"Mostly."

They both glanced at the colt.

"I pray he'll make it, Mom."

"So do I. We all do." She gently stroked Jay's hair. "You go and use the washroom. I'll stay with Snowfall."

Jay hauled herself into her wheelchair. "Did I see Shane here last night?"

"What makes you say that?"

"I don't know if I was dreaming. But he was sitting on that old saddle in the corner and watching me. It sure looked like him."

Her mother smiled. "You can ask. Shane and your father are eating in the kitchen."

As soon as Jay wheeled into the kitchen, her father got up from the table, wiping his mouth with a paper napkin.

"Roll on up and have some waffles and strawberries," he said.

Shane turned in his seat, a sausage on the end of his fork. "Yeah, Jay, sit with us for a bit."

"I can't," she replied. "I have to get Snowfall drinking."

"Start with apples," suggested Shane. "I think if he'd take a small apple, that would whet his appetite for something wetter and juicier. Remember my mare High

Five? She was doing poorly one fall and wouldn't take anything into her mouth. But she finally ate an apple, and from then on she was okay with food and water."

"I guess I'll try that. Thanks for watching over me last night."

Shane smiled. "Watching over you?"

"I saw you sitting on the busted-up saddle in the corner."

"It wasn't me."

Jay smiled back and almost stuck out her tongue. "Then I guess it was an angel."

Dad walked to the counter and poured himself a cup of coffee. "They arrested one of the shooters in the next county. Whatever he said was enough to send the FBI to Reynolds' ranch. He's in custody now."

Jay's emerald eyes flared. "I hope they hang him!"

"Well, if he's convicted he'll face jail time and have to pay a hefty fine. Hefty even for him."

"None of that will bring back the Mustangs he shot."

"Justice never brings anything back. It just gives you a chance to start again."

Jay reached for a basket of apples and took out the

smallest ones she could find. "Can I keep Snowfall?"

Her dad nodded. "I expect there'll be some paperwork and payment involved. But we can look into it."

"If he can step on his left leg without much pain, I hope we can get him up today."

"Don't rush it."

Snowfall wouldn't take Jay's apples. Pastor Luke visited in the afternoon and prayed with her and the colt. The yearling perked up a bit, sniffed something on Luke's jeans that interested him, and lay his head back on the hay. Luke rubbed his hands and an apple over the spot and offered the fruit to the colt. He sniffed it, nibbled at it, and suddenly took the whole apple into his mouth, chewing and slobbering.

"Quick!" exclaimed Jay. "Give him another, give him another! But rub it over your jeans first!"

Luke took two more apples, ran them up and down over his pant leg, and offered them to Snowfall. The colt actually sat up on his hind legs to eat them. Jay reached up from her chair and gave the pastor the last three apples.

"What's on your jeans?" demanded Jay.

"I have no idea." Then Luke grinned. "I was at the

Penners' home before I came here. Their paint Salsa Q leaned her head over the fence and wanted to be scratched between the ears. She pushed her head into my chest. Now that I think of it, I guess she pushed it into my legs and knees too."

"See if Snowfall will take those three apples. Then you could rub the water bucket and see if he'll drink."

"That sounds crazy, Jay."

"Pastor, I don't care if it sounds crazy. I just care if it works."

Snowfall ate the final three apples, saliva pouring out of his mouth and over his jaw, and when Luke brought the bucket close to his head, the horse hesitated, struggled, and pushed himself up until he stood. He wobbled, favored his left rear leg and lifted it off the ground, but he remained upright and dipped his head to drink. He was so thirsty he knocked the bucket out of Luke's hand.

"Fill it up again!" cried Jay. "There's a tap just outside! Hurry before he loses interest!"

Luke scrambled outside. Jay heard water running into the empty bucket with a roar, Snowfall stared intently at the doorway, and the pastor returned, lugging the bucket in front of him and offering it to the colt.

Snowfall wasn't any gentler as he drank the second time, but Luke held onto the bucket more firmly. Just as the colt finished, Jay wheeled herself to the barn door and pulled it shut.

I don't want him running away.

Strangely, Snowfall didn't panic, even though he was in a barn and had two humans next to him. He swung his head from side to side, kept his left rear hoof off the barn floor, sniffed at the hay, and started eating.

Pastor Luke pulled his cell phone from his pocket and walked a few feet away.

"Who are you calling?" asked Jay.

"Your mom and dad. They have to see this. Then I'm going to call the vet."

"Why don't you just go to the house and get my parents?"

"No, I'm not leaving you alone with the colt. Maybe he's feeling doped up now, but he's still a wild horse. He could start running and kicking and who knows what."

"Not Snowfall. If you had seen him out on the range you'd know what a chicken he is."

"I'm staying with you."

"All right."

The sun rose in Jay's chest again. She watched Snowfall chewing the hay, now and then lifting his head to glance at her. She wished she could turn cartwheels or somersaults, she felt so good inside. *Thank you, God. If I never walk again it's all right because we saved Snowfall. Just let him stay with us. Please let him stay with us.*

The colt did stay with them. His wound healed, any jitters he had about being around humans never surfaced in an aggressive way, and Jay slept beside him night after night. Every now and then she turned over to see Shane watching her from the old saddle.

*****

"He's going to be a pony," Charlie told Jay after one of his checkups on the colt six months later. "His muscles are developing well, he's got all the strength he ought to have, but he's not going to get much bigger. He's not going to top fourteen hands."

Jay bit her lower lip. "Are you sure? He had such long legs when he was a foal."

"But look at him now. Thicker mane, coat, and tail,

thicker neck, his bones are getting heavier, his barrel wider, and you can see for yourself his legs are much shorter now in proportion to the rest of his body. He's a beauty, he's got that look about him, and the copper/gold of his coat is something to see, isn't it? But he'll be a pony. Not a weakling, understand that, Jay. He'll work as hard as any full-grown horse, and even your brother or your father will be able to ride him."

But not me. I still can't walk.

*****

Over the next two years, doctors tried different operations and used steel pins in Jay's bones, but she never reached the point where she could move on her own without crutches or her chair. Her sixteenth birthday was bittersweet, for her friends and family and church gathered at the ranch to celebrate, and that was good, and Shane led Snowfall around the corral closest to the house, the horse groomed and braided as if for show, and that was good too. But when Shane rode him through the gate and out into the nearby fields while people clapped, the sun in her chest disappeared, and a thick cloud took its place.

I still sleep beside him now and then. Feed him oats and apples

out of my hands. Brush him down and make sure his mane and tail
are free of burrs. But others chase the wind and gallop him through
the sage. I guess it was better for me before he was broken to the bit
and saddle, when he was still young and wild. Then I was the same
as everyone else—a watcher and an admirer. Now anyone in the
world can climb up onto his back except me.

"I can lift you into the saddle," her father told her when
the party was over and the last pickup had pulled away
from the house.

Sitting at the kitchen table in her wheelchair, Jay
nibbled at a cookie. "You'll really let me ride him?"

"If you're not in too much pain. I don't know if your legs
and hips can handle it. I doubt you can grip his flanks."

"So what will you do? Lead me around the corral as if
I'm five years old?"

Her father poured coffee and didn't answer.

She threw down the cookie and wheeled herself up the
ramp to her room. "Forget it. I can't walk. I can't ride. I can't
do anything. You treat me like I'm a child. I'd be better off
dead."

Jay had scarcely banged open the door to her bedroom
when her father called, "Slapp Reynolds, you remember

him?"

She paused before entering her room. "Of course, I remember him— the murderer. He did less than a year in jail."

"But he also had to do three years of community service with equestrian clubs and events. He's coming by tomorrow."

"Why are you letting him onto our property?"

"He's visiting us so he can see Snowfall."

"That monster is not going to see Snowfall!"

"It's the law. Reynolds has to see him and help with his care for a couple of weeks."

Jay almost launched herself out of her wheelchair. "A couple of weeks? That man is not laying a hand on my pony! Not a hand! He can go back to jail and spend his two weeks there!"

"Jay, give him a break. He's been living with this for more than two years. They say he's a changed man."

"Who says that?"

"Why, Pastor Luke for one. He meets with him for coffee and counseling every week. And the boys at the Bar Cross say the same thing. He spent a month with them."

Jay's face flushed red hot. "He's just doing that because the judge said he had to! And he's smooching everybody up and saying the right things so the judge'll go easy on him and let him out of all this community service early! Dad, why do you let a man like that fool you?"

"Jay, people can change. You know that. We talk about it every Sunday in church. Jesus talks about it."

"We talk about wolves in sheep's clothing too, don't we? And that's what he is, and none of you can see it!"

Jay wheeled herself into her room and banged the door shut with her hand. Seething, she glared through her window at the sun setting purple in the west. *I should just get on Snowfall tonight, no matter how much it hurts, and ride away from all of them, from Dad and Mom and the people who love to see Shane riding my horse, and ride away from Slapp Reynolds too. I don't care what some judge says. He's not putting a finger on my pony. Not ever.*

Mom came in and sat on the edge of the bed. "Did you enjoy the party?"

"Most of it," said Jay.

"We need to have your girlfriends over more often."

"Why? I don't have anything in common with them

anymore."

"Of course, you do. All of you love horses."

"Yes, ma'am. We can spend hours talking about riding them. The trouble is I can't get on a horse anymore, so once that part of the conversation comes up, I have nothing to say. It makes for great friendships. Sitting and listening to others talk. Sort of like sitting in a wheelchair and watching others ride."

"There are other things you can talk about, aren't there?"

"Sure. We can talk about boyfriends. Except they all have boyfriends, but I don't, so once again I sit on the sidelines and watch and listen. My life has become a spectator sport, Mom."

"Nonsense. All kinds of boys are interested in you."

"Who?"

"Hank Thompson. Jerry Braun. Sid Carter."

"Oh, yes, Hank and Jerry and Sid. My cell phone rings day and night. They text me without stop."

Mom grasped her daughter's hand. "They were here for your birthday."

"They were here to hang out with Crystal and Brie and

Taylor. Not me."

"That's not true."

"Of course, it's true. I'm sixteen, and I've never been kissed. I'm a loser, Mom. I can't walk, I can't ride, I can't drive a car. I'm nothing. I've got no friends left, and no boy comes within twenty feet of me. There's nothing left to live for, okay?"

Her mother tried to smooth back Jay's hair, but her daughter turned her head away.

"You're beautiful, Jay. There's going to be a young man in your life one day."

"Yes, I'm stunning, aren't I? I'm the Queen of the Silver Dollar. No man can resist my charms. My eyes just pull them in. The line-up stretches from here to Cheyenne and way beyond to Santa Fe."

Her mother released a frustrated sigh. "You were never one to complain. What changed?"

"What changed is nothing changed. Disappointment wore me right down to the ground."

Mom's eyes fell on the Bible lying open on the bedside table. "You still believe in God don't you?"

"He's about all I've got left outside of my family. I'm

sorry, Mom, I love you guys, I really do, but it hasn't been a good day for me, so I'd rather be left alone…if you don't mind."

"Can I pray for you before I say goodnight?"

"Whatever."

Her mother prayed, Jay closed her eyes and prayed her own prayer, and while her words and her mother's words mingled in her mind, she imagined getting on Snowfall and riding right of the county, right out of the state, and, if possible, right out of her world. *What if I could disappear up into Canada? Just keep going and never stop until I found an old abandoned cabin in the woods, one with a stream and a meadow right beside it where Snowfall could graze and get a drink? Or suppose I rode south through Mexico and down into Paraguay and Ecuador and Argentina? It's warm there, and it wouldn't be hard to live off the land. Or maybe I'd ride west to the ocean and a take a ship to Hawaii. They cowboy there too. I've read about it. Snowfall could handle the voyage if I had enough hay and oats. Oh, Lord, I'd just like to start again, have a brand new life, be a brand new person in a brand new place. Help me, please, help me. Somehow I need to crawl out of this skin and have a second go at everything.*

That night Jay couldn't sleep. At two o'clock, she slowly

and silently wheeled down the ramp and eased out the back door to the yard. Making her way into the stables, she spoke softly to the horses in their stalls, but none of them nickered. Snowfall rubbed his head against her, and she kissed him. She reached up and got a blanket on the pony, as well as a saddle, and tried to mount, using a stirrup and the horn. But pain ripped through her legs and hips, and she thought she was going to pass out. She fell back into her chair.

"Well, I'm not giving up," she said, gritting her teeth. "Lord, I have to start my journey now, this morning. My new life is champing at the bit. But I can't get anywhere if I can't get on my Mustang."

Again, she reached up from her chair for the stirrup and horn, but the pain made her flinch, and she fell back. There was a third attempt and a fourth attempt, but she still couldn't get into the saddle. Tears of frustration stung her eyes. Finally, with all her strength, she launched herself like a rocket, landed on the seat of the saddle on her stomach, but went too far, slipping over on the other side, striking her head on a wooden post, and lying unconscious in Snowfall's stall.

The horse sniffed and nuzzled her face and neck,

standing over her as he slept.

*****

"Are you all right? Excuse me, are you all right?"

A hand gently shook Jay's shoulder.

She opened her eyes.

A young man was kneeling beside her, black Stetson on his head, brown eyes deep, soft, and concerned.

"Who are you?" she asked.

"I'm Garnet. Your dad said I'd probably find you in here sleeping with your pony. But it looks to me like you took a nasty crack on the head." His fingers touched the bump on her head. At his touch, a shiver ran up Jay's spine. She took in her breath so sharply, his brown eyes grew even more concerned.

"Can I do anything to help you?" he asked. "Can I carry you into the house?"

"I'm—I'm trying to get on my pony."

"I can get you up there." He put his arms under her. "Put your arms around my neck so you're steady."

Without arguing, she did as he asked, and he lifted her off the hay as if she were a piece of straw.

"Don't spread your knees too much," he said. "Just keep

them tight to your pony. It won't hurt nearly as much if you do that."

She hardly felt any pain as he placed her in the saddle. "How do you know?"

"I've been helping injured riders get back into riding for the past two years at clubs all over the state." He patted her lightly on the back. "You sure look awesome up there. You and the palomino suit each other. Just a sec." He took a red paisley scarf from his jean pocket, dipped it in a bucket of water nearby, wiped a thread of dried blood off the side of her face, and smiled the biggest and brightest smile Jay had ever seen on a man. "Pretty as a picture," he said. "Now you can go for a ride, Miss Price."

Pain stabbed at her knees, but she ignored it. She was on a horse.

She was on her pony.

It felt to her like she was on a mountaintop.

"Thank you, Garnet. I'll do just that. I'm grateful for your help in getting me into this saddle." She took a deep breath. "And for putting me on a wild horse for the first time in my life."

"You're welcome, Miss Price." He took a good look at

the way she was sitting. "Hey. Your knees are way too doubled up."

"I like it that way."

He began loosening her stirrups. "Maybe you did before your fall. But you'll have to get used to a different way of riding if you're going to stay in the saddle." He stopped and smiled up at her. "Is that okay?"

She smiled back. "Yeah, it's okay. How do you know so much about me?"

"I asked around."

"Why?"

"Because I knew we were coming to your ranch to help out."

Jay closed her eyes and opened them again. "You're a Reynolds, aren't you?"

"That's right." He finished with one stirrup and moved around to adjust the other, one hand on the Snowfall's backside as he walked around behind the pony. "Do you want me to leave?"

Jay stared at him a long time without replying.

He loosened up the second stirrup and stood back, staring at her.

"I know what my father did," Garnet said. "I also know he sees everything in a different light now. He's up at the ranch house with your mom and dad if you want to talk to him."

"I don't think I'm ready for that yet."

"I understand. He and I fought when the shooting happened. I mean, it was a bad fight. It's behind us now. I did all his community service with him. You should know we intend to keep it up. As far as we're concerned, there is no deadline. We're going to keep on working with the equestrian clubs and the wild horses."

"Is that just you talking?"

"Nope. It's my old daddy talking too." He tapped her lightly on the leg. "It was a miserable season in my family's life when he did what he did. I don't blame you for not believing him when he says he's sorry. But I can say he's born fruit in keeping with repentance, like the Bible commands."

Jay raised an eyebrow. "Like the Bible commands? I've never seen you at church."

"Well, there's more than one church."

"What's yours? Lutheran? Episcopalian?"

He smiled again.

At the smile, all the walls she had built against intimacy, as well as against his family, walls she had spent years constructing, came tumbling down.

And she smiled back at him—without meaning to or wanting to.

"The hills and mountains, Miss Price," he answered. "The blue sky. The meadows where the Mustangs graze. It suits me."

"Don't you miss people of like mind and like faith?"

"Sometimes. Do you have an indoor church you'd recommend?"

"Please call me Jay."

"I like Miss Price."

"No one talks like that anymore, Garnet."

"Maybe not. But you're a lady, and the title fits."

A surge of heat flushed her cheeks. "I'm no lady."

His face became as strong as the mountain river running through the middle of the Price ranch. "Yes, you are." A smile opened his face again. "They told me a lot of things about you when I asked around. What they didn't tell me was what a beauty you were. Miss Price it is."

The heat in her cheeks turned to fire.

Garnet touched his fingers to the brim of his hat. "You take care as you ride. And head past the house so your folks can see you."

"I'm not sure, you know. Not sure I'll be able to stay in the saddle."

"Just walk Snowfall. Keep your knees pressed in. Talk to him. He's been gentled by your voice. You'll do awesome. You're a brave woman."

"You seem to know so much about me, but I know so little about you."

Garnet shrugged. "Not much to tell. Born, grew up on a horse, never got off him, riding him still. He was a Mustang once too." He walked beside her as she nudged Snowfall out of his stall and out of the stables. "One step at a time, Miss Price. How does it feel to be up there?"

It seemed she had smiled more with Garnet around just a few minutes than she had at any time over the past two years, and now she felt herself smiling again. "It feels like what I imagine heaven will be like. The things you can't do, you can, and you're not afraid anymore...or you're not down... just happy. That's all I am right now. Happy."

"Happy as a mountain bluebird." He tugged at the brim of his hat. "Except you're a redhead, so I guess I'd better change the bird to something like a cardinal. This Reynolds won't disturb you any longer. Walk your pony around the yard and take your time. Blow us all a kiss when you reach the house. I guarantee you everyone will run outside and cheer you in a snap of your fingers."

"They'll run outside, all right. And they'll most likely order me to get off Snowfall or tell my brother to take the reins and lead me around as if I were a child at the state fair." Jay stared intently at Garnet. "Would you ride with me?"

"Me? A Reynolds?"

"Yes, you a Reynolds. Your father took part of my life away. I want you to help me get it back."

"How do you expect me to do that, Miss Price?"

Jay gathered the reins tightly in one fist. "They said I'd never walk again. So I won't walk. I'll run."

"What?"

Jay kicked in her heels, swallowed the pain it caused, and bent close to the pony's neck as the Mustang exploded across the ranch yard in a flurry of dust and hooves. As they raced past the house, Jay caught a glimpse of her father standing with a cup of coffee and an open mouth and her mother's eyes springing wide and staring. Then Jay went through the gate and tore across a flower-speckled pasture. Snowfall's mane streamed back in Jay's face. Then she turned to look behind her.

"Are you coming, Mister Reynolds?" she called.

He had already brought their black, The Color of Night, out of the stables and had leaped onto the gelding's back, not bothering to use a saddle or reins, knotting his fingers in Color's shining mane, galloping after Jay.

Racing, she looked skyward, her red and gold hair falling loose over her shoulders, and laughed in a way she had not laughed in years.

The pony reached the rail fence at the far end of the pasture.

"I can't climb down to open the gate, Snowfall," she said as they thundered toward the fence. "You're going to have to jump it. Never mind me. I can take it. I'll cling to you like a second skin. Let's go!"

Garnet, pounding over the grass on The Color of Night, shouted at her to stop, but his cry caught in his throat as he watched the pony clear the fence, land, and carry on as if the morning wind had swept out of the mountains and was carrying pony and rider with it. He heard Jay sing out her thanks to God and urge her pony to go faster and faster. Jay and her palomino dashed through red and orange poppies and through meadows that ran a thousand miles to the sea. Garnet knew he might never catch up to them, but he began to laugh as the hard ride took the wind out of his lungs.

"A woman with that kind of spirit," he said to the gelding, "is only going to come around once in a lifetime. I don't care if we have to ride all day and all night and wind up in the California surf. You've got to get me that girl, my friend."

Jay's voice echoed back to him over the green fields. "Have you given the horse strength? Have you clothed his neck with thunder?"

He shouted back as loudly as he could. "Their horses are swifter than leopards! They fly like an eagle!"

She reined in her pony.

In seconds, he was by her side.

Nostrils flaring, the gelding and the pony were lathered in sweat.

"Why did you stop?" demanded Garnet between breaths. "I thought you'd take us to the ends of the earth."

"I stopped because this is easily one of the best days of my life, Mister Reynolds. I didn't expect it. I can't believe what's happening, and I feel as free as a skylark."

"But that jump you took over the fence. It must have hurt."

"At first. When we landed, it shook all my bones. But you know what? I can handle it. It's okay. It really is."

"You're pretty amazing."

"I'm amazing? You hardly know me and I'm amazing?"

"What I know so far, yeah, you're awesome."

"That's sweet of you. It makes the day a little bit better than it already was." Jay hesitated, looking at him. "But there's one thing missing to make it wild and beautiful and complete."

Garnet wiped his forehead with the back of his hand. "What's that?"

"You won't do it."

"Of course, I'll do it. Why wouldn't I do the next crazy thing? I practically broke my neck chasing you over this field."

Her green eyes glittered. "Kiss me."

"Kiss you?"

"God's given my life back to me. He's let me run, he's let me breathe, he's let me laugh. But I've never been kissed."

Garnet stared at her in surprise. "Are you kidding me?"

"Am I that bad?"

"No. I can't believe my luck is so good. God sure smiled on me when I woke up this morning."

She smiled. "So is it a yes?"

The smile came that made the sun rise in her chest and blaze like golden fire.

"It's yes a thousand times," he said, his voice growing quiet.

"Then go ahead. I've got my breath back."

Garnet drew Color closer, reached over, and placed his left hand under her head, sliding his fingers through the crimson and gold tangle of Jay's hair, softly placing his lips on hers.

She closed her eyes and a mixture of thankfulness, excitement, and sunlight moved through her like a stream flowing freely through white mountains. He pulled away, but she brought her hands up and tugged his mouth back to hers, kissing him a second time.

"Sixteen and never been kissed," Garnet whispered, continuing to hold her close.

"Not anymore." She smiled into the soft brown eyes she had woken up to that morning. "How about you?"

"Nineteen and pretty much the same. Every guy's first kiss should be like this."

"And every girl's."

"Do you hurt from the riding?"

She snuggled her head onto his chest, and his arms went gently around her. "I don't feel any pain at all."

Hush a bye

Don't you cry;

Go to sleep my little baby,

When you wake

You shall have

All the pretty little ponies.

Paint and bay, sorrel and gray

All the pretty little ponies

Hush a bye

Don't you cry;

Go to sleep my little baby,

When you wake

You shall have

All the pretty little ponies,

All the pretty little ponies.

STORY THREE

Lauren's Dream Horse

Melodie Parker

"Easy Blaze, it's just a deer." Lauren Davidson gave the startled mare a pat on the neck as a deer darted across the trail and bounded into the woods.

A flood of memories poured into Lauren's mind as she dismounted and walked to a wooden cross at the top of a lonely hill. The cross marked the spot where her first horse, Jameelah, had been buried thirteen years ago. Ellen and Kathy Connor, sisters and Lauren's two riding buddies, sat quietly on their mounts...waiting.

Most people would describe Lauren Davidson, a tall thin gal with hazel eyes and long, dark hair, as shy and reserved, but those who were closest to Lauren knew of other facets of her personality. She could also be fun-loving and adventurous. Her mother would quickly testify that

Lauren, so very young at heart, never acted her age while growing up.

"Are you coming, Lauren?" Ellen asked. "We should be going."

"I think I'll stay here for a while. I'll catch up with you later."

"Okay," Ellen called over her shoulder as their horses cantered away. "See you back at the barn."

Lauren allowed her mind to wander into the past when she was about eight. She wanted a horse so much and thought it had to happen, or she couldn't stand it. She recalled the painful memory of the day when her mother finally made it clear there would be no horse.

"Lauren, there is no way we can ever get you a horse. I know you really want one, but we live in town and don't have the right place for it. We can't afford to board it. The monthly fee is just too expensive."

Often, when she was alone in her bedroom, Lauren cried her eyes out. How could God deny her a horse when she wanted one so much?

As the years passed, Lauren had the opportunity to ride a few times a year. Rachel and her mother, friends at church, had invited Lauren to learn to ride their two horses, a time in her life she never forgot. Lauren also read every book and magazine about horses she could get her hands on. She made and sold tack and accessories for model horses and used the profits to buy horse things for a "horse hope chest." Although Lauren saved some money for riding lessons when she was fifteen, she only took two because the instructor seemed more interested in chatting with a friend and only pointed out Lauren's mistakes. Lauren felt like a failure, and her parents already had had enough of the instructor's attitude.

"How long do you expect us to keep bringing you here?" Mom asked. "Why do you need lessons when you already know how to ride?"

Lauren remembered how hurt she felt. Nobody seemed to care how much she loved horses, and nobody understood that in order to ride well, it took instruction and practice. Would anything ever work out? Lauren felt like she had to wait forever for anything she really wanted, and owning a horse was no exception.

Like a lot of young ladies, the dream of a horse went on the back burner because of romance. Lauren fell in love with a boy when she was sixteen. They eventually dated and got engaged. But the relationship didn't work out, and Lauren had an even worse heartbreak to face than being denied a horse. It was during that time Lauren realized she was focused on what she wanted and not really seeking what God wanted. This experience drove her to her knees and into a deeper relationship with her Lord and Savior Jesus Christ.

A loud snort from Blaze brought Lauren back...to the present...to the horse she now rode.

"I can't believe how fast time has flown, girl."

The mare lifted her head from grazing and nickered as if to say she agreed. On a slow walk back to the barn, Lauren's mind turned again to her thoughts.

When Lauren was twenty-five, she finally earned enough money at her factory job to afford a horse. Although she longed for a place of her own, she continued living with her parents to save money.

"I'm so afraid something is going to prevent it again, Lord," Lauren often prayed. "Please show me clearly if it's not the right time for a horse."

The right time to buy a horse meant having a place to keep it. But where do I look? Lauren prayed, and God seemed to answer.

Near Lauren's home, a beautiful farm stood that Lauren loved since she was a little girl. With the farm less than two miles away from her house, Lauren drove there to talk to the owner. Much to Lauren's surprise, the farm boarded horses.

"I never had a horse of my own and don't go riding," explained Mrs. Shaffer, a friendly woman in her 60s, whom Lauren immediately liked. "I just enjoy taking care of the horses. I do the morning feeding and turn the horses out. Then the owners are responsible for the evening feeding, cleaning stalls, and purchasing feed and bedding. Farrier and veterinary care are also the owners' responsibility. I can't promise a stall will still be available when you get a horse. I never know who's coming and going."

"I understand, Mrs. Shaffer," Lauren said. "I really hope I can board here. The boarding fee is very reasonable, and I have dreamed of keeping a horse here since I was a little girl."

Another feather in Lauren's horse-owning cap occurred

when a Christian camp she attended offered riding lessons.

"We offer, private, semi-private, and group lessons," Sandy, a woman with a friendly voice, said when Lauren called for information. "Yes, we offer both English and western lessons. We do ask you to take a private lesson for your first time so I can evaluate your riding and get an idea of your experience."

Although Lauren had learned to ride western, she decided to take English lessons to become as well-rounded a rider as possible.

"Please let riding lessons be a positive experience this time, Lord," Lauren prayed as she drove to her first Friday evening lesson. Pulling into Sylvan View Stables, Lauren broke into a sweat, and she felt butterflies in her stomach. Her glance focused on a large Appaloosa gelding tied in the corral. A slender blonde woman came out of the barn and approached Lauren. She extended her hand warmly and gave Lauren a friendly smile.

"Hi, I'm Sandy, and you must be Lauren. It's very nice to meet you." Sandy led Lauren to the gelding tied to the corral fence and introduced Apache. "We brought him with us from Maryland when we moved here," Sandy explained.

"He's a good lesson horse."

"Is he the one I'll ride?" Lauren asked, immediately recognizing Sandy's love for horses.

"Yep, Apache is your mount." Sandy pointed to a small Arab mare in a nearby paddock. "And out there is Angel. She's my own personal horse not used for lessons much, but I just couldn't part with her."

"Oh I absolutely love Arabians," Lauren said. "In fact, I hope to own one soon. I'm going to be looking for a horse, but I thought I probably should have a year of lessons first."

"A lot of people don't like Arabians," Sandy said. "They think they're too spirited and sensitive, but I love them too. Well," she said, turning toward the Appaloosa, "let's get started."

Lauren faced the left side of the horse and paused. "Oh, this will be different. No horn on the saddle."

"Right. There's no horn," Sandy said as she helped Lauren mount. "Use your legs and your balance to hold on. And hold the reins taut. That's different too. No neck reining here!"

"O-okay, I'll try my best." Lauren felt a knot in her stomach as she realized Sandy's observing eyes would continually be watching.

"Give a little squeeze with your heels when you're ready to go." Sandy slowly backed away. "Move him over to the rail and just walk for now to get the feel of him. Heels down, chin up."

A few walks around the ring and Lauren reversed her direction, still staying along the rail.

"Try not to pull your hand too far to the side!" Sandy said, demonstrating the proper direct reining technique. "You're doing really well, Lauren. Now we're going to try trotting."

Finally, Lauren began to relax and enjoy herself.

"Now, I want you to come off the rail and make a circle toward the middle of the arena, then go back along the rail, and continue going the same direction. Try to make your circles as perfectly round as you can."

Lauren tried her best, but she had a lot to learn. Her circle was not perfectly round, and Apache slowed to a walk halfway through the circle. Lauren clicked her tongue and squeezed her heels. With that little nudge, the horse picked up a steady trot again.

"That's it! Keep him going," Sandy said.

I wish Mom could see me now, Lauren thought. *There certainly is more to riding a horse than just sitting on a saddle!* Lauren couldn't believe how fast the hour passed. Definitely a positive experience this time around!

"I have good news for you," Sandy told Lauren when the lesson ended. "There are four levels of riding according to the Certified Horsemanship Association. I consider you a Level Two rider."

"Wow," Lauren said, laughing. "I'm glad I'm at least one level above the bottom."

*****

"I'm so happy for you!" Lauren's friend Rachel said. "You've waited so long. I'm glad you're taking riding lessons and finally able to look for a horse."

Lauren finally had the time to spend a weekend with her long-time friend Rachel at her apartment. Since they now went to different churches and Rachel was in her fifth and last year of college, Lauren hardly saw her anymore. No wonder Lauren couldn't wait to see Rachel and reminisce about the fun times they had as kids.

"Rachel?" Lauren said as the two got ready for bed.

"Huh?" Rachel, said, her eyes heavy with sleep.

"I feel so left behind. I mean, here I am twenty-five-years old, still unmarried, no desire for a career, and I'm still trying to fulfill my dream of owning a horse. I feel like life is passing me by. Because of everything that's happened in the past, I can't help but wonder if something will stop me from getting a horse again."

"Don't worry, Lauren. I know God has nice young men for us to marry, and you'll get your horse. You're too determined not to, and God knows our hearts and the desires we have. It'll happen in His perfect time."

"God's time sure is a lot slower than my time would be, but thanks for your encouragement."

Whether Rachel's right or not, she always seems to know the right thing to say. "Good night," Lauren called to her friend who had curled up on her bed across the room.

"Good night, my friend, and sleep tight."

*****

A few days later on her way out the door at home, Lauren said, "Hey Mom, if you happen to talk to your friend Becky sometime, could you please ask her if she knows anyone who has Arabian horses? That's the breed I am looking for."

"Well, since she owns horses, she might know something, so I'll ask her, but are you sure you should do this?" As usual, Mom had reservations about the horse situation.

"I've waited forever, Mom. Now I can finally afford one. Yes, I'm sure. I've prayed about it, and the Lord hasn't shown me any reasons not to pursue it."

Several days later, Mom, at last, had a positive report for her daughter. While Lauren relaxed in her bedroom after a hard day's work, her mother yelled up the stairs. "Lauren, I talked to Becky today. She said she has a friend who breeds Arabian horses, and she has one for sale...if you're interested. I wrote down all the information."

Lauren bolted down the stairs, took the information from Mom, and read it: "The horse is a black mare, fourteen years old, and very quiet. If interested, call Julie McAlister."

"Julie McAlister!" Lauren said. "I know her...I mean I don't really know her, but I used to work with a relative of hers. I forgot she breeds Arabians."

"Well, Becky apparently knows Julie really well. She spoke very highly of her. She said Julie is an animal lover, a super nice person, and completely trustworthy. Becky also said she would meet us at the McAlister farm when you want to take a look at the horse."

"That's just awesome! I'll call Becky in a little while."

Later that evening, Lauren spoke to Becky on the phone.

"So you like spirited horses," Becky said in the midst of conversation.

"Well, yes, and I think Arabians are just absolutely beautiful."

"Beauty isn't everything. I have an Arab mare, and she is quite a handful. I love her, though, and I know what you mean. They are beautiful."

Lauren briefly considered what Becky had said. Maybe Becky worried about Lauren's lack of experience. *Oh well,* Lauren thought, *the mare is fourteen. Her spirit should be toned down by now. Besides, her temperament is quiet.*

Two days later, Lauren and her mother drove down the long driveway of a beautiful farm. Lauren smiled as she drove, pleased as punch her mother had come with her just for moral support. Lauren glanced out the window as she parked near a large stable. Beyond the stable were rolling hills of pasture with several grazing horses. A gorgeous chestnut Arab stallion paced in his paddock and whinnied at the mares nearby.

When Lauren and her mother got out of the car, Becky greeted them. She led them into the stable where they met Julie who stood, brush-in-hand, by a black mare with a shiny coat, large eyes, and delicate pointy ears so characteristic of an Arab horse. Lauren's gaze swept over the entire horse, noting the concave profile of the mare's head, the arched neck, and refined "China Doll" stature.

"You must be Lauren and Mrs. Davidson," Julie said, smiling.

"Yes," Lauren said, as she walked to the mare. She carefully slipped her hand under the mare's muzzle and allowed her to smell.

"It's very nice to meet you both," Julie said. "This is Jameelah. Her name means 'beautiful' in Arabic."

"She certainly is beautiful," Lauren said.

"Becky tells me you've been taking English riding lessons."

"Yes, I learned how to ride western when I was ten, but I haven't had much chance to ride over the years. I felt I needed more riding experience before getting a horse."

"Great," Julie said. "Jameelah doesn't neck rein, so it's

good you're taking English lessons. We're retiring her from breeding, and my husband feels we have too many older horses here. We need to use our space for broodmares, so we want to find her a good home. Unfortunately, though, you won't be able to ride her today," Julie added. "The details are a little sketchy, but one day while we were away, the neighbor's dog got into the horse pasture and chased the horses. Jameelah stepped into a groundhog hole as she was running and severely strained her flexor tendon and suspensory ligament. She seems perfectly sound now, but I decided to have the vet double-check things. He felt she should have a full year of rest from being ridden. I was a little surprised, but I decided it would be best to do what he said."

In two seconds, Lauren's whole horse world fell apart. She had her heart set on this horse the moment she saw her. And, besides, there weren't that many Arabians for sale in central Pennsylvania.

But then, Lauren's spirit soared when Julie said, "If you're still interested in a year, we'll keep her for you, but if you want to look at other horses, that's fine too."

"Oh, I am definitely still interested," Lauren said in a

matter-of-fact tone. "It will give me a chance to get more riding experience under my belt."

"Would you like to walk her around a bit?"

"Sure," Lauren said.

Julie hooked a lead shank to Jameelah's halter, which had a small chain looped over the mare's nose. "She should be fine, but just in case...." Julie gestured toward the chain shank.

Lauren led the mare behind the barn, the horse's gait so fluid it seemed like she was floating. Jameelah carried her head high, her nostrils flaring as she sniffed the air. She looked all around, whether from anxiety or curiosity, Lauren couldn't tell. Then the mare broke into a slow trot, threatening to gallop, but Lauren got her back into a walk with a slight jerk on the chain, a turn in a circle, and a firm command to walk.

"How'd she do for you?" Julie asked Lauren back at the barn.

"Very well," Lauren said. "She's quite a beauty."

"Whenever I sell a horse, I like the prospective owner to spend as much time as possible with it to know if it will be a good match or not," Julie said. "I'd like you to come as often as you like to groom Jameelah and take her for walks. Can you do that?"

"I certainly can...and I certainly will," Lauren said as she stroked her soon-to-be dream horse.

*****

The weeks and months passed. Lauren continued to improve with her riding lessons and even had jumped some low cross rails. She kept her word and went to see Jameelah as often as she could, walking and grooming the mare. Although Jameelah had the quiet demeanor with "nice manners," she sometimes showed a flair of stubbornness by pushing her nose into Lauren's chest if she was annoyed or impatient. However, a sharp word from Lauren would immediately stop the behavior. And when Jameelah spooked while walking behind the barn, Lauren had no problem calming the horse down. "At least she spooks in place and doesn't flip out," Lauren said to Julie.

"I have something really special to show you," Julie said one day and gave Lauren a copy of Jameelah's pedigree.

Curious about the horse's roots, Lauren got a book about legendary Arabian horses and found two that were in Jameelah's bloodlines, Fadjur and Bask. "Wow," was all

Lauren could say as she studied the book one evening at her kitchen table.

"What are you reading?" Mom asked.

"A book about famous Arabian horses, and Jameelah's related to some of the horses in this book!"

"What does that matter?"

"It means she has really great bloodlines! It means….oh never mind," sighed Lauren. *No use trying to explain anything "horsie" to a mother, who has no interest in equines.*

*****

Almost a year went by when Lauren received a phone call from Julie. "The vet gave the okay, and I rode Jameelah today. She did well, and there was no sign of lameness. Come tomorrow and try her out."

Lauren could hardly sleep, waiting for the next day to arrive. After work, she went home and changed then went straight to see "her horse."

As she climbed onto Jameelah's back, Lauren had the same butterfly feelings she had at her first riding lesson. "Please don't do anything stupid," she muttered under her breath. She began by walking the mare then urged her into a trot. Lauren did some posting and then tried riding in the two-point position. However, Jameelah decided to lower her head, which nearly pulled the reins out of Lauren's hands.

The result?

Lauren lost her balance, flew over Jameelah's head, and hit the ground with a thud. "So much for not doing anything stupid," Lauren grumbled as she struggled to stand.

"Are you okay? What happened?" Julie asked.

"Ugh...I don't know. She put her head down, and I lost my balance. But I'm not hurt."

Lauren swallowed her pride and decided she would just do "regular old riding" and not try to impress Julie. It quickly became obvious Jameelah only understood basic cues. She tossed her head in irritation when she didn't understand something Lauren asked her to do. Lauren knew and accepted the fact that Jameelah was not trained like the lesson horses. She also knew they both needed a lot of work.

After a month of riding Jameelah, Lauren made the decision to make Jameelah officially her own. Over the past year, Lauren counted the horses grazing at the Shaffers' farm every time she drove by, fearing she would see five horses, which meant all the stalls would be filled. Thankfully there were only two horses at this time. "I'll be purchasing a horse very soon," Lauren informed Mrs. Shaffer.

In a few days, Lauren anxiously called Julie, realizing her dream was coming true with the big responsibility that came with it. Deep down inside, Lauren worried how Jameelah would respond to new surroundings but quickly shoved the worry away.

On a hot Saturday in early July, Julie pulled into the Shaffers' driveway with Jameelah in tow. Jameelah came out of the trailer with sweat dripping off of her. "She has always done well in the trailer before, but today she kind of got worked up a bit," Julie commented.

Lauren walked Jameelah around the farm and then put her in her own pasture to get acquainted with her stablemates with a fence in between. The other horses came running when they saw the newcomer. Jameelah explored her surroundings and then stood under a tree. Julie and Mrs. Shaffer, acquaintances, talked with each other as Lauren approached them.

"I hope Jameelah will be okay," Lauren said. "She isn't

even grazing."

"I'm sure she'll be fine," Mrs. Shaffer said.

"It'll take her a little while to get used to her new surroundings," added Julie.

Before leaving the farm, Julie said, "Don't be afraid to call anytime with questions or concerns. I would be glad to help you with anything. Enjoy her and take good care of her," she said, climbing into her truck.

"I will," Lauren said. "You bet I will."

*****

At church on Sunday, twelve-year-old Charity Connor came to Lauren, a big smile on Charity's face. "I heard you got a horse!" she said. "I love horses!"

Charity was one of seven children, whose family owned another nice farm near Shaffers' place. Lauren knew the Connors had a horse and hoped someone in the family would go riding with her.

"My sister, Ashley, has an Appaloosa mare named Lady, and she goes riding with our neighbor across the ridge," Charity said. "There's a bridle path beyond the ridge Ashley will love to show you."

"And I'll love to learn about it," Lauren said.

After a few days, Lauren led Jameelah out of the barn. Mrs. Shaffer stood leaning against the fence, watching her horses graze.

"I think it's time for Jameelah to pasture with the other horses," Lauren said to Mrs. Shaffer. "I just hope they don't kick each other and get hurt."

"I'm sure they'll be fine," Mrs. Shaffer said again. She swung the gate open, and Lauren released her horse into the pasture. Mrs. Shaffer closed the gate, and the women stood watching the horses chase each other, a normal activity for horses to get to know one another. Jameelah looked beautiful with her arched neck and flagged tail. Lauren burst with the pride of owning such a beautiful horse.

But beauty isn't everything. Unfortunately, over the next few months, Lauren found those words to be true of Jameelah. It seemed the more Lauren rode her, with other horses or by herself, the more uncooperative the horse became. She needed coaxed to go on certain trails, she sidestepped when Lauren tried to walk her on roads with traffic, she chafed at the bit, wanting to go back to the barn, and one time she stopped in the middle of a road and wouldn't budge, bringing the traffic to a standstill. When

Jameelah started spooking at chipmunks, deer, or any movement on the trail, Lauren decided to call Julie.

"Hmm....maybe horses actually get worse as they get older," Julie said.

Lauren wasn't sure Julie was joking or serious, but either way, the horse's dangerous behavior was something new for Jameelah.

"She never acted that way before," Julie continued, "but it's been a long time since we did any trail riding or took her along any roads."

Lauren wondered if Jameelah had become used to her life of leisure and didn't want to be ridden anymore or if something had happened to make her fearful. Maybe Lauren herself was instilling fear in the mare without realizing it. Lauren kept all these thoughts to herself. "Try using a riding crop to tap her rump whenever she decides to swing it out like that," Julie suggested.

But that didn't appeal to Lauren at all. As she continued to ride Jameelah, Lauren tried everything to help the horse behave, all to no avail.

On a cool day in late September, a day Lauren will never forget, she came home from work and decided to go for a ride by herself even though Jameelah had been doing better with other horses. Uneasy and a little bit unnerved, Lauren still hoped for a relaxing ride through the woods to enjoy the early changing leaves. The first hints of gold and yellow dotted the rolling hills all around.

But Jameelah was having a bad day, which added to Lauren's uneasiness. Right from the start, the mare fought the bit and stepped away when Lauren tried to cinch the saddle.

Frustrated, Lauren spied her riding crop in the tack room and picked it up. "Don't give me a reason to use this," she said.

After managing to tack the horse, Lauren mounted, and the pair headed down the road, but Jameelah balked almost immediately. At the end of Shaffers' property, Jameelah tried to wheel around and head back to the barn.

"Oh, no, you don't," said Lauren. "How can we enjoy ourselves if you're going to fight me the whole time? I can't let you get away with this."

Whack!

The sound of the crop striking Jameelah's rump seemed to echo. Just then, Lauren felt a surprising jolt that scared her. She realized Jameelah had bucked. She had never done that before. Nerves on edge, Lauren felt like giving up because Jameelah was so jittery and uptight. Lauren got her calmed down as best she could and wished she had not used the crop.

"If we go back to the barn now she will think she is being rewarded for bad behavior," Lauren said to herself. Lauren dismounted and led the mare down the road toward the bridle path. The lane bordered the Connors' property. Lauren thought about stopping to see if Ashley could go riding but decided against it. "You have to learn to go without other horses," Lauren said to her Jameelah.

But the ride turned into disaster. Jameelah jumped and snorted at everything. Things that never usually fazed her were a big deal today. Jameelah felt like a time bomb ready to explode. When a chipmunk chirped at them from the underbrush, the mare spooked and tried to run from it. Lauren soon decided it was time to head back before Jameelah became even more unglued. "What's wrong, girl?" Lauren asked as she carefully mounted her again. "What in the world is wrong?"

Jameelah had worked herself into a sweat by the time

they got back to the barn. Lauren dismounted, loosened the cinch of the saddle, and walked Jameelah to cool her out. They walked behind the barn when, suddenly, Jameelah planted her feet, raised her head and began snorting nervously.

"Easy girl," Lauren said. "It's okay." But Lauren might as well have talked to a tree. Jameelah snorted again, looking toward the woods along the ridgeline.

Lauren looked in that direction but could see nothing. Expecting the mare to freeze in place and then calm down like she always did, Lauren never could have prepared herself for what happened next.

Jameelah lunged forward and began running a circle around Lauren at the end of the lead rope.

"Whoa, whoa, easy girl. It's okay." Lauren spoke as calmly as she could.

The mare had a terrified look Lauren would never forget. Jameelah's eyes were huge as she started grunting, and her mouth opened wide. She started bucking as though a demon had climbed on her back!

Lauren surveyed the area again but saw nothing that would be so frightening to a horse. "Whoa, whoa, easy!"

Lauren said but to no avail.

For a few brief seconds, Jameelah stopped, but then she started running and bucking again. Afraid the horse would trample her, Lauren let go of the rope, hoping the mare would run to her stall.

In the split second she let go of the rope, Lauren remembered the blacktop area surrounding the barn entrance. It was very slippery for hooves, especially for a horse running at full speed. Lauren watched in horror as Jameelah started slipping as soon as her hooves touched the road. Lauren's stare was glued to the mare's previously injured leg.

"She's going to break her leg! She's going to break her leg!" Lauren screamed.

Then Lauren heard a sickening crack. Almost paralyzed with fright, Lauren managed to run over to the mare, who had fallen hard, examining every inch of her body. But the horse's leg wasn't broken. Instead, Jameelah had hit a post of the rail fence bordering the Shaffers' driveway and cracked her head open.

"Oh, Jameelah, Jameelah!" Lauren cried, her heart torn to shreds.

The mare, lathered in sweat, lay with her eyes wide open, her jaw gaping.

Weeping, Lauren bent down and touched Jameelah, but the horse did not respond. Lauren stroked the horse's neck and knew in the depths of her heart that Jameelah, her dream horse, was dead.

*****

In time, Lauren's broken heart began to heal, and she was able to accept she would never have all the answers to her questions regarding her beloved Jameelah. About eight months after Jameelah's death and with all Lauren learned from the experience, she felt ready to look for another horse.

Arabian horses would always be her favorite, and she knew there were some "quiet ones" for sale in the area, but Lauren decided to seek the first "bombproof" horse she could find, no matter what breed it was. Searching horse sales on the Internet, she found an ad for a Morgan mare. The advertisement stated the horse was fifteen years old and a beginner's horse. "Sounds just what I'm looking for," Lauren said to herself. She sent an email to the owner, who responded promptly with a picture.

"You won't be disappointed," was the statement in the

email. The picture showed a pudgy chestnut mare with a little boy sitting on her back.

"Maybe this is the horse for me," Lauren told her mother before she made the forty-five-minute trip on a Saturday to check out the mare named Blaze.

Things went well when Lauren rode her in the arena, but she wondered how she would be on the trail.

"She doesn't bat an eye at traffic," stated Heather, the owner. "She isn't one to spook much. She's trained English and western and has been used for lessons. Her previous owner used to take her to shows, although I'm not sure what kind of showing they did. She's a little headstrong, so I always use a curbed bit when I ride her. We're selling her because we just have too many horses."

"And now you have a buyer," Lauren said.

For Lauren, it wasn't love at first sight with Blaze like it had been with Jameelah. The first time Lauren brushed Blaze and tried to put a fly sheet on her, Blaze swung her head around and nipped at Lauren.

"I don't know about this horse," Lauren complained to her mother later that day. "Today she tried to bite me. She doesn't like hugs or anything being tight around her. I think she doesn't like me."

"You've only had her a few days," Mom said. "She's probably just getting used to things. Give her a chance."

Lauren's mouth hung open in dumbfounded silence. Was this really her mother speaking—the person who usually had only negative things to say in regard to horses? If her mother was saying something positive related to this horse, then Lauren thought she should listen.

"Okay," Lauren said, "I'll give her a chance."

*****

Lauren had Blaze about a month but just didn't feel like she had bonded with the mare.

"What's the problem?" Lauren prayed. "Is she not the right horse for me, Lord?"

But in that still small voice, the Lord impressed upon Lauren that she was comparing Blaze to Jameelah instead of loving Blaze for who she was.

"I'm sorry, Lord," she prayed. "I'll try to do better."

It took about three months, but Lauren did bond with the mare. Lauren got to know her new horse's quirks and what to expect from her. Soon she formed a love for Blaze as much as she had loved Jameelah. Blaze proved to be a faithful mount and companion in the years that followed. Because of Blaze's sweet disposition, Lauren discovered she had regained her courage to work with another "dream horse" the Lord had sent her way.

Next to Jameelah's grave, Lauren stood and dusted herself off. Now a woman of thirty-nine years, she had been married for seven years with three small children. With such a young family, Lauren knew her horse owning days had come to an end. Blaze, now twenty-seven, had started to show her age with grey hair on her face and arthritis in her knees. Sadly, Lauren and her husband could no longer afford to board Blaze, so Lauren gave her to the Connors.

Although welcome to ride Blaze anytime, Lauren wondered if she would ever own another horse again. If not, she still thanked God for the many years she had the privilege to own and enjoy not one, but two, of God's most wonderful creatures on earth.

"Thank you for allowing my dream to come true, Lord," Lauren whispered as she looked heavenward and nudged Blaze forward. "C'mon, girl. Let's head back to the barn."

Darkness Before Dawn

Brenda K. Hendricks

Late for the evening meal again, Dawn Williams rushed into the dining room where the other family members were already engrossed in conversation. She plopped onto a chair at the Victorian cherry table and wiped her clammy forehead with a napkin then placed it onto her lap. Thankfully, air conditioning offered welcome relief from the August heat.

Dad sat at the head of the table in perfect posture. A few grey hairs, which according to him Dawn had caused, stood out against his otherwise mousy-brown hair.

She forced a smile. When he didn't return it, she braced

herself for another lecture on tardiness.

"You're fourteen years old, Dawn." He always began by reminding her of her age, as if she'd somehow forgotten. "It's about time you learned the importance of punctuality. Proper etiquette includes …."

She had tried. She really had. But she found separating herself from Sundance for any reason to be the most difficult thing she'd ever had to do.

Her twenty-year-old brother Zeke winked at her, then he scooped a huge mound of mashed potatoes onto his plate and smothered it with beef gravy. His mane of dark blond, wavy hair stood in stark contrast to Dad's styled-to-perfection do. Why didn't Dad ever correct Zeke for his table manners? Surely proper etiquette had something to say about that.

Mom dabbed the corners of her mouth with a napkin. Her auburn hair pulled off her neck in a loose ponytail accented her dainty features—features Dawn wished she'd inherited. Although there was no mistaking their deep dimples, the wave in their hair, and oval faces, Dawn was painfully aware of her own larger frame. Mom ate expressionlessly except for her hazel eyes, which twinkled in amusement, whether at Zeke or at Dad, Dawn couldn't be sure.

"Punctuality shows respect and marks character." Dad continued.

Dawn smiled, musing over her horse, golden coat shimmering in the sun as she'd groomed him moments ago. How she loved that animal. She still had trouble believing Dad had finally permitted her and Mom to each get a horse after years of coaxing. They had the best time riding together every day. And Dawn had planned a great surprise for Mom tomorrow.

"This conversation amuses you?" Dad's voice broke through her thoughts.

"No sir." Dawn twisted a strand of her silky, dark-brown hair to inspect for split ends. She fashioned her long, thick locks into a knot on top of her head, securing it with a rubber band.

"Furthermore, how many times do you have to be told not to fuss with your hair at the dinner table?"

Mom passed the roast beef to Dawn. "Douglas, didn't you lecture enough in the courtroom today?" Good 'ole Mom often interrupted Dad's rants, somehow managing to turn the evening conversation into a barrage of jokes and laughter.

Dad cleared his throat and looked at Dawn. "Yes, we do have other matters to discuss. As I was telling your mother and Zeke, I've arranged my schedule so that we could have some quality family time before Zeke returns to college."

"Family time? As in a vacation?" Dawn sipped at her sweet tea.

"Yes, indeed." Dad's face brightened with a broad grin. It looked good on him. Too bad he didn't use it more often. "I've made all the arrangements. We leave for the lodge in the morning."

"What?" Dawn almost choked on a mouthful of green beans. "Tomorrow? But I had a surprise for Mom."

"Dawn, dear." Mom reached across the table for Dawn's hand, almost toppling her glass of tea. "I'm so excited that you have a surprise for me. You're such a sweetie. Can you maybe give it to me after we do the dishes?"

"The surprise will take too long."

"Can it wait until after our vacation?" Dad asked. "We'll only be gone four days."

"Four days?" Dawn pushed her empty plate away, her

stomach twisting into knots. "Can I take Sundance?"

Dad shook his head. "We don't have a horse trailer. Even if we did we couldn't take him. It's a fishing lodge. It doesn't have stables."

"Then I'm not going." Dawn folded her arms.

"Of course, you're going," Mom said. "We haven't had a family vacation in such a long time. I'm sure there's plenty of wildlife…makes for a great photo shooting experience."

"Sharon." Dad scowled. "Stop entertaining her childish notions of wildlife photography. She'll attend an ivy-league school, of her choice of course, and become a lawyer or doctor or—"

"I don't want to make occupational decisions tonight." Dawn sighed. "I just want to carry out my own plans for tomorrow's surprise." She gave Mom her best please-help-me look. "I discovered a really sweet trail we've never ridden together."

"That sounds wonderful, honey." Mom scraped and stacked plates. "We can do it the day after we come home."

"Dawn, the world doesn't revolve around you and those horses." Dad scrubbed his mustache with a napkin and turned to Zeke. "We'll go fishing upstream while the girls sun themselves and swim. Just like old times."

Zeke nodded. "Sounds great." While chugging his sweet tea, he shot a sympathetic glance at Dawn over the rim of his glass.

"Good. Then it's settled," Dad said. "We'll leave at daybreak. After we check in at the lodge, we'll hike to the river with our fishing gear and bagged lunches prepared by the lodge, of course." He looked tenderly at Mom. "I don't want you to have to lift a finger during this vacation, dear. We'll return to the lodge by dark-thirty each evening." Dad's sad attempt at a joke bombed as usual. "Except for Monday. We have to check out by one, but if we get up early, we can still get some fishing in."

"Dad." Dawn sat up straighter to please him. "Can't we at least compromise? You're a lawyer. Compromise is the name of the game."

"Sounds like a winning idea." Zeke smiled. "We could leave...say at three-ish. That way Mom and Dawn could go on their ride. And we'd have plenty of time to fish in the evening."

"Sorry, not this time." Dad stood and pushed his chair under the table. "We have to be at the lodge by ten or we lose our reservations."

"Please, Dad, can't you call the lodge and change the time?" Dawn pouted. "I promise I'll never be late for another meal as long as I live. Just let us have a morning ride. Please."

"It doesn't work that way, Dawn. I really am sorry, but I can't change that part. The lodge's rules, you know." Dad walked into the living room. Dawn matched his step, hoping to find a loophole in his plans.

"But Dad, who's going to take care of Sundance and Charlie while we're gone?"

Dad sat in his easy chair and buried his nose in the evening paper.

Dawn waited a split second for a reply. When none was offered, she said, "I guess I better stay home and take care of the horses then. I'll go tell Mom."

"You're worrying too much." Dad lowered the paper. "I've arranged for Mr. Dixon to tend to them."

"Mr. Dixon? Sundance has never met him. What if they don't get along?"

"I guess you'll have to teach your horse some etiquette as soon as you learn some yourself. Now go upstairs and pack."

Dawn left the room in a huff, stormed through the kitchen barely noticing Mom at the sink, and slammed the back door. She kicked a stone down the path that led to the barn. Grazing next to the fence, Dawn's registered Palomino gelding nickered and nodded his head, melting her heart and taking the edge off her frustration. Far out in the field, Charlie, a black Quarter Horse, lifted his head and whinnied.

She slid the barn door open and stepped inside where Sundance met her. She tossed a saddle over his back and secured the bridle around his muzzle, giving him a kiss on his velvety nose. She led him out of the barn and mounted him. With a gentle nudge to his ribs, Dawn coaxed him into a gallop. They raced around the perimeter of the fence as one—the best feeling in the world. Strands of Dawn's hair loosened from the knot on top of her head and whipped across her face. For hours, she enjoyed the sense of real freedom until the stars shone overhead in full array. A slight tug on the reigns slowed Sundance, signaling him to return to the barn.

Inside, Dawn removed the bridle, hanging it on a nail in the post and then hoisted the saddle onto the divider between the stalls. Even more reluctant to leave Sundance than normal, she brushed him an extra-long time.

"Four days away from you." Dawn hugged Sundance's neck, soaking his mane with her tears. "I think I'll die."

Reluctant to take her eyes off him, she backed out of the stall, settled into a pile of straw, and cried herself to sleep.

*****

"Honey, wake up." Mom gently nudged Dawn.

Dawn yawned and rubbed her eyes. Sundance nickered and gently nibbled at her hair. Mr. Dixon's rooster crowed in the distance. "Mom? Sundance? Did I sleep in the barn all night?"

"You sure did. When you didn't come in by bedtime last night, I came looking for you.

You were already sound asleep. I figured since you're going to be away from Sundance for so long, it wouldn't hurt to let you sleep out here."

Dawn stretched and yawned again. "Thanks, Mom." She suddenly jumped to her feet. "Oh my goodness. I'm not packed. Dad's gonna be so upset." She brushed the straw off her clothes and hair, hugged Sundance's neck an extra-long time, and then kissed his nose. "I love you so much and miss you already. Be good for Mr. Dixon. I'll see you in four days, okay?"

"Come on, honey," Mom said, hurrying out of the barn. "We better get moving."

Arm in arm, Dawn and her mother raced into the house. At the top of the stairs, they parted ways—Dawn to the bathroom and Mom toward Dawn's room.

"Hurry and get your shower. I'll bring your clean clothes to the bathroom and pack for you. Anything in particular you want to wear?"

"No. I'm fine with whatever you throw in for me. Who's going to see me anyway, right? Would you make sure my camera's in my backpack, please?"

"Will do."

"I'll take your stuff down and load it in the Jeep," Mom called down the hall.

"Thanks."

As she showered, Dawn fought the gloomy mood that threatened to squelch the family vacation. Four whole days away from Sundance. *It just isn't fair.*

Dawn stepped out of the shower, dressed as slowly as possible, and trudged down the back stairs to the kitchen where Zeke sat at the breakfast bar, dipping toast in an egg.

At the stove, Mom looked in Dawn's direction and winked. "Good morning, sunshine."

She slipped an egg and two pancakes on a plate. "Is over-well okay?"

"Sure." Dawn forced a smiled and slid onto the stool across from Zeke. "It's the only way to eat eggs."

"Come on, Kidstuff, give us a real smile." Zeke laughed then chugged his orange juice. "We'll have a great time." Dawn loved him to the seventh galaxy and back. He was the best big brother ever. But she'd still rather spend the next four days with her horse than go on this fishing trip.

"I don't see why Mom and I even have to go," Dawn mumbled through a mouthful of pancake. "You guys will fish the whole time and not even know we're around."

"Dawn, are you starting with the attitude already this morning?" Dad said as he filled the doorway with his frame and the entire kitchen with his presence. He was a big man, but he didn't intimidate her, not really. Most of the time a little pouting brought out the hidden pussycat—the lion suppressed inside. But then there were times like last night when she and her father went at it with claws extended, and neither of them would back down until they both crept away licking their wounds. *Why can't we get along like Mom and I do?*

Usually the light of the new day refreshed their mutual respect and understanding. But not this time. Dawn wasn't ready to give up...not just yet.

Mom set a plate on the breakfast for Dad. He sat next to Dawn and said, "It's such a beautiful morning. I took the top off the Jeep before I packed it. I figured we'd all enjoy the fresh air. We'll leave as soon as I finish my breakfast."

Dawn suppressed a sigh. This family fishing trip seemed ludicrous. And spending four days away from Sundance was most definitely unbearable. From the time she had gotten him six months ago, not a day had gone by that she hadn't spent every minute of free time with him...grooming him, riding him, admiring him. If she had to suffer, she'd make sure her whole family would feel her pain.

As soon as Dad took his last bite, Mom grabbed his plate from the table, placed it in the dishwasher, and pressed the "On" button. "Time to hit the road," she declared.

Sometimes that upbeat attitude of Mom's drove Dawn nuts. It was contagious. And the last thing she wanted right now was an upbeat attitude.

They all rushed out the back door and piled into the Jeep Wrangler like one big happy family…almost. As they drove down the lane, Mr. Dixon rounded the corner in his rusty pickup, heading toward the barn and Dawn's horse. Dawn sighed, slumped in her seat, and closing her eyes, pretended to sleep.

Per her norm, Mom started to sing, "Off we go into the wild blue yonder…."

Zeke harmonized with his baritone voice. After the third goofy song, Dad added the bass. Although it didn't sound half bad, Dawn sank lower into her seat and held her ears shut, determined not to join in the fun.

At precisely 9:35 A.M., Dad swung the Jeep around the circular driveway and parked in front of an overgrown log cabin with a wrap-around deck complete with a dozen wooden rocking chairs and checkerboard tables. Leave it up to Dad to pick an old folks' retirement home for a summer vacation.

Everyone grabbed their gear and followed Dad into the lodge. Mounted fish, bear, and deer heads, as well as ducks and turkeys stared at them through glass eyes. Dad rang the buzzer for the clerk.

A young, blue-eyed, blond man with shoulders almost as broad as Dad's welcomed them with a friendly smile.

Dawn immediately forgave the gorgeous hunk for the creepy "stuffed" greeters and smiled back.

After taking care of registration, the clerk ushered them to their suite, informed them of the rules and regulations, bid them a good day, and moseyed down the corridor.

At least I'll have someone almost as handsome as Sundance to occupy my time. My knight in shining armor. I wonder if he owns a white steed. Never mind. Dad plans to leave for the river as soon as we unpack. We wouldn't get back until "dark-thirty." Tomorrow at "quarter before daybreak," we'll head out again and repeat the cycle for the duration of our vacation. I'll probably never see the cool desk clerk again. So much for a budding relationship.

Mom clasped Dawn's hand and walked her across the family room. "This will be your room. Isn't it homey?"

Homey? What did that mean exactly? Plain? Without a view? "I want the room with the door to the deck."

"Zeke's in that room, dear."

"Why does Zeke always get the nicest room? It's so unfair. I had to give up my plans and my horse. Can't I at least have the room with the deck?"

"I don't see what difference it makes since we won't be here much. But you have given up your plans for this trip, and I know the surprise meant a lot to you. I doubt if Zeke cares about the room. Let's go ask."

"Thanks, Mom." Dawn followed her mother to the bigger bedroom. Zeke had already stuffed the dresser drawers with his belongings and was inspecting his fishing lures.

"You wasted no time moving in." Mom said with that "cup of cheer" voice of hers.

"Yup." Zeke glanced up then returned his focus to his tackle box. "I'm about ready to head to the river. What's up?"

"Would you mind switching rooms with Dawn? She'd like the one with access to the deck…you know, to unwind and think when we get back from fishing."

Zeke gave them a quizzical look. "She'll have all day to unwind and think. What does she need the deck for? Besides, I have all my stuff put away."

Dawn put on her best puppy-dog-pouty face, the one Zeke never could resist. "Please, Zeke. I'm the one getting the short end of the deal here. Don't I deserve some sort of compensation for everything I had to give up for this trip? I'll help you move."

"I wish you would've said something sooner." He closed his tackle box and sighed. "I guess I can do that much to accommodate you since you gave up so much. But I don't see what difference it makes. We'll only be here to sleep."

"That's what I tried to tell her, Zeke." Mom stretched to kiss his cheek. "You're such a good man. Thank you."

Dawn tossed his clothes into the suitcase, closed it, and gave her brother a peck on the cheek too. "Thanks, Zeke."

As she arranged her clothes in the drawers in the bigger room, a timid knock broke the silence. Mom stepped just inside the doorway. "Dawn, I hope switching rooms helps to make the trip more enjoyable for you. Time to get out of your mood and have some fun, don't you think?" Without waiting for a response, Mom turned and disappeared into the adjacent room.

Mom has a point. This is a beautiful lodge, well…except for the staring animals—and the grounds hold a lot of potential for adventure and great photo shoots. But I miss Sundance so much.

*****

With a backpack full of food for the day, Zeke led the way over rocks and mud puddles on the trail to the river. Carrying the tackle boxes and fishing rods, Mom and Dad strolled together with hands clasped, engrossed in conversation. Dawn missed her horse even more. She adjusted her own backpack and swatted at the pesky mosquitoes and gnats. Bugs in these woods had no respect for generic insect repellent.

As a squirrel scurried along an oak branch, he chattered a warning to the passersby.

Dawn snapped several shots of him and deliberately waited until the others were out of sight. Although the mysteries of the forest tempted her to wander, she moseyed down the beaten path, snapping close-ups of wild flowers. At the bend, Dad sat on a boulder. A breeze tussled his hair, making him look unprofessional… even carefree...and Dawn giggled.

"You shouldn't linger so far behind us." Dad smoothed his hair back into place. "You'll get lost."

"I'm staying on the path."

He slid off the boulder. "There are bears and snakes around here."

"Great for photographing."

"They might not like posing. What if they turn on you?"

"And how are you going to protect me, Dad? Snag the bear in the ear with a fishhook and reel him into court for a fair trial?"

He grinned. "You're becoming quite witty, young lady, like your mother."

"Thanks. I'll take that as a compliment."

"As intended."

They strolled down the path, picking up the pace with the conversation. When the others came into view, Dad slowed to a leisurely walk. "Dawn, I'm sorry this trip is so boring for you. I should've thought to invite one of your friends. I just assumed you'd be content to spend the time with your mother."

Dad apologizing? Really? I must be dreaming. Soon I'll wake to Mr. Dixon's rooster crowing, and Mom and I'll meet in the barn to saddle our horses and ride.... "Ouch!" Dawn cracked her big toe on a rock.

Dad grabbed her arm, preventing her from sprawling out on the ground. "Are you all right?"

"Yeah."

"You're even acquiring some of your mother's grace. You looked a little like a floundering fish there for a minute."

Dad actually chuckled. It was almost worth tripping to hear him laugh. "Gee, thanks." She shook off the embarrassment as he released her arm. "It's not that I don't want to spend time with Mom or any of the rest of you. I just really miss Sundance."

"I don't understand your obsession with that horse. He's all you think about. Maybe being away from him will help you refocus."

"How could you understand my love for that horse? You hate animals." Dawn ran ahead to catch up with the others.

"I don't hate horses. Dawn…." Dad's voice trailed after her.

Twigs and leaves crunched behind her, signaling his approach. He caught her arm and stopped her in her tracks. "Dawn, please," he said through deep breaths. "I admit I'm not an animal lover, but I don't hate your horse. I just want to have family time like we used to."

"I may be obsessed with my horse. But you're just as

obsessed with your work. You're seldom home. I miss you."

Dad softened his tone. "That's exactly why I scheduled this trip. Will you please try to enjoy our vacation?" He released his grip and trudged down the path.

Dawn followed, adjusting her mood to include the guilt that now mingled with the frustration. I'm really trying to have a good time. *But all I seemed to be doing is making everyone else as miserable as I am. And how can I not be obsessed with Sundance? When I ride, our spirits intertwine as though I become horse and he becomes human—one and the same, totally united, inseparable. There's no other feeling like it this side of...of the seventh galaxy. I guess I am obsessed with that four-legged beauty. But is that so wrong?*

When Dawn and her father reached the river, Mom and Zeke had already fastened a tablecloth on a dilapidated picnic table and had set the boxed lunch in the center. Mom waved, and Dad returned the greeting. Dawn crossed her arms and pursed her lips.

"I found this little chipmunk." Dad swung his thumb in Dawn's direction. "She was wandering around, lost and scared. Do you have any nuts for her?"

"Looks like I'll be eating with a few nuts," Dawn said,

trying to join the fun.

"I don't know about nuts." Mom draped an arm around Dawn's shoulder. "But we have plenty of grub. Come, little chippy." They walked to the table. Mom sat then patted the seat beside her.

As Dawn perched on the bench, Zeke unpacked the basket. "This is like a Christmas surprise. We've got foot-long ham and cheese hoagies." He pulled four sandwiches out of the cool pack. "Cole slaw, cubed watermelon, cantaloupe, and honeydew," he added, placing each container on the table. He set the cool pack and box on the ground and sat across from Dawn. "I'm starved. Let's chow down!" He grabbed a hoagie, unwrapped it, and bit into it as though he hadn't eaten for a week.

The food disappeared quicker than the squirrel Dawn had photographed on the trail. Zeke licked the last drops of mayonnaise from his fingers, grabbed his fishing gear, and headed upstream.

Mom tossed the garbage into the trashcan and walked over to the riverbank. "The water seems a little high for this time of year."

Dad joined her. "I don't know. If so, not much. Don't

worry. We'll stay within earshot." He gave Mom a quick kiss on the forehead and hurried after his son.

Dawn sat on the grass and leaned her back against an oak tree about fifty feet from the river. "Mom, do you believe in tree hobs and sea monsters?"

"Where'd that silly question come from? You know there are no such things."

"How do you know? You said once that you believed in angels and demons."

Mom leaned against the tree next to Dawn. "I do believe in entities as such. You know, Dawn, over the past twenty years or so, I've done a lot of searching for spiritual truth. I was raised in a Christian home. But when your dad took me out of that environment, I discovered there were a whole lot of other belief systems out there. I doubted what I had been taught as a child and experimented with new disciplines."

"Really?"

"Yeah. All religions hold a measure of truth, but most of them hold a lot of fear and uncertainty too. I've come full circle. Christianity replaces fear and uncertainty with hope and assurance. It's hard to explain."

"But how did you come to the conclusion that

Christianity was right?"

"Zeke and I were having a discussion on world views and religions. I was surprised at his vast knowledge of belief systems including Christianity. Among other things, he pointed out that if men had made up the story that Jesus rose from the dead, they never would've said the first person to see him was a woman."

"That's silly. Why not?"

"In those days, women weren't considered credible witnesses and weren't permitted to testify in a court of law. Men fabricating a tale like Jesus' resurrection never would've used a woman for a witness. Yet, several women saw the resurrected Jesus before any men witnessed the Living Son of God. I've been reading the Bible again and feel so full of life. I've been waiting for the right time to tell you and your dad about the Lord."

Mom often burst into song and dance for no particular reason. Today was no exception. She stood and pulled Dawn to her feet. For the first time today, Dawn willingly released her sulkiness and clasped Mom's hands. As they twirled in circles, their dark hair swirled in the breeze. Memories of past fishing vacations flooded Dawn's mind with happiness.

She hadn't realized how much she missed being a little girl...and these moments of sheer pleasure. They twirled and sang silly songs until they both collapsed in a dizzy, giggling heap.

"Oh Dawn, I have so much to share with you." Mom said breathlessly. "I believe Jesus is who he claimed to be, the Son of God, the Savior of the world...my Savior."

Mom's words muffled as Dawn's mind drifted back to Sundance. He was probably grazing in the lower pasture wondering where she was and why they hadn't gone for their morning ride. Would he ever forgive her for leaving him with Mr. Dixon?

"Come on, Dawn." Mom slipped off her tennis shoes and jumped to her feet. "Sundance is fine. Let's go wading with the ducks."

Mom always seemed to know what Dawn was thinking to the point that Dawn wondered if she could ever have a private thought. "Do you think I obsess over him?"

"Not any more than I obsessed over my first horse." A subtle smile crossed Mom's face. "Which was a lot, now that I think about it." She pulled Dawn's shoes off and yanked her to her feet. "Nothing like a cool dip in the river to cure the horse aches. I'll race you."

While Mom darted to the water's edge, Dawn plodded after her. Although shallow at the edge, the water deepened toward the middle of the river, crashed against a huge rock, and swirled around the opposite side.

Ankle deep into the icy river, Mom laughed as she kicked a hefty spray of water. It drenched Dawn all the way to her waist, causing her to shiver.

"C'mon, honey, get out of that grumpy mood. The water's exhilarating." With another kick, Mom slipped and fell backward.

Dawn waited a heartbeat for her mother to stand. "Mom, quit clowning around…Mom?" Another heartbeat, Mom drifted motionlessly away from shore.

"Mom!" Dawn plunged into the water, straining every muscle in her legs. "Mom! Get up." Caught in a fast current, her mother's body floated farther downstream.

"Dad! Dad!" Dawn swam with all her might, screaming and paddling, but the current kept her mother just out of reach.

Seemingly out of nowhere, an arm stretched around Dawn's waist and pulled her back to shore.

"Let me go! I have to get to Mom." She kicked and flailed, trying to free herself.

"Dad has her! Settle down!" Zeke said as he set Dawn on the shore. He sat close and wrapped his arms around her. Together they watched Dad carry their mother's lifeless body to shore.

"No! Mom! Zeke...Mom!"

*****

Awakened by her own screams, Dawn wiped her sweaty face on her pillow, rose from her bed, and stood by the window. A ribbon of pink streaked across the dark sky. How dare the sun continue to rise! She had enjoyed watching the start of each new day from this window. She had looked forward to all the promises each day held. She had found happiness in most everything. But that was...a lifetime ago.

The sun peeked through the treetops, and long shadows stretched across the pasture. If she'd open the window, she'd hear Sundance's whinny. She pulled the drapes shut and crawled back into bed, too numb to care. A gentle tap on the door interrupted her solitude.

"Go away and let me sleep."

"I brought you breakfast." The door creaked as Dad opened it. He crossed the room, set the toast and orange juice on the nightstand, and sat on the edge of the bed. His bloodshot eyes betrayed his lack of sleep.

"Dawn, you haven't been outside since...," his voice cracked "...since your mother's funeral two weeks ago. The beginning of next week, I'm going to have to resume my work, at least in part."

"I know."

"I need to know you'll be all right."

"I'm fine."

Dad shook his head. "You haven't even been to the barn to see Sundance."

"I can't go there, Dad." The knot in Dawn's throat tightened, and she swallowed hard. "It's too difficult. It was our dream to have horses...Mom's and mine. What good is a dead dream?"

"It's not the horse's fault, you know. If you'll just go see him again, he can help you through this."

"I can't."

"I'll go with you."

"But you hate the barn and the horses."

"Hate? It's such a strong word."

Dawn shook her head. "I don't want him."

"What? You begged nearly all your life for a horse."

"Just…just get rid of him."

"I've made arrangements to take your mother's horse to the livestock auction at the end of the month. Why don't you give it some serious thought until then?" Dad kissed her forehead and left the room.

Time passed in a torturous rhythm of days and nights as an indescribable emptiness engulfed the house. Dad's face grew thin and ashen. Zeke opted to skip a semester of college and accepted a job with a construction firm. Dawn wished she could skip the rest of her life. Although she woke before daybreak as usual, she didn't bother opening the curtains. What was the point? Her stomach churned as she tightened her belt to take in the excess fabric of her shorts.

A faint tap on the door announced another wasted sunrise…another breakfast.

This time Zeke opened the door a crack before entering. "You up?"

"Yeah, come in."

He set the tray on the nightstand and sat on the bed.

"Thanks, Zeke." Dawn took a sip of orange juice then replaced the glass. "Where's Dad?"

"He's feeding the horses."

"Dad?"

"Yeah, we've been taking turns since I started working and have to leave earlier than he does."

"So why haven't you left?"

"I'm taking the day off to spend with you."

"With me? Why?"

"Today's the day…." Zeke's words slipped out cautiously as he opened the curtains. Dawn squinted at the brightness of the sun and quickly yanked the curtains shut.

"You don't have to do this, Dawn. If you'd just go down and say goodbye to him."

"I can't, Zeke. I hate him. I want him out of my life forever."

"I don't believe you. That horse means the world to you."

"Meant…past tense. He meant the world to me until Mom—"

"It was an accident."

"An accident that never would've happened if I hadn't

been obsessing over that horse. She fell backward into the water, trying to cheer me up. Who knew a large rock under the surface stopped her fall?" Still clinging to the curtains, she clenched them until her knuckles turned white. "I'll never love anything or anyone like that ever again."

"It wasn't your fault, Kidstuff. Please let it go." Zeke pried her hands loose and pulled her trembling body into a brotherly hug as she wept.

Finding comfort in her brother's embrace, Dawn took a deep breath, gently released his grip, and backed away. "I'll be all right…really. I just need some time alone. Okay?"

Zeke nodded, his moist eyes full of concern. "We love you, you know." He turned and walked out of the room.

An hour later, Dawn peeked through the curtain. An unmarked horse trailer pulled up to the barn and stopped. The driver and a passenger jumped out. Dad and Zeke greeted them with handshakes.

It really was happening. She had given permission for Sundance to be sold with Charlie. Soon the horse she had begged for all her life would be gone forever.

She raced down the stairs. By the time she stepped out the kitchen door, she caught a glimpse of the trailer as it turned the bend. She ran to the end of the fencerow and trudged back toward the barn.

Dad met her halfway, wrapping his arm around her shoulder. "Are you okay?"

"No…no, I'm not okay, Dad." Wiping away her tears with the back of her hand, Dawn nestled into his embrace. "I'm sure I made the right decision, at least for Sundance. He deserves more than an empty heart incapable of loving him."

Dad kissed the top of her head. "That's a very mature attitude, honey. But you're being very hard on yourself."

She sighed. "Will this pain ever go away?"

"I've heard it gets easier with time." Dad whispered as they walked across the yard and into the kitchen.

"So I've heard."

*****

Time proved to be a slow healer. On more than one occasion, Dawn thought she'd heard her mother's laughter or singing. Once, Sundance's whinny called her to the barn. Nothing but devastation and emptiness met her there.

By mid-October, Dawn opted to do an in-depth study on world religion for school, not so much for the extra credit as to find answers to personal questions.

Dawn stepped off the school bus, ran a finger over the top of the For Sale sign at the end of the lane, and plodded along the fencerow to the house. Instead of going directly to her room, she slipped into Dad's study—a virtual library with shelves of law books on two walls. On the third wall were Mom's books—fiction, self-improvement, cookbooks, and what piqued Dawn's curiosity the most, volumes of religions of the world. Two shelves full.

"Dawn."

She swallowed hard and turned. "Zeke! What are you doing home?"

"We finished the bridge early. What are you up to?"

"I'm working on a world religions project for extra credit in world cultures."

"Sounds intriguing." He strolled across the room, sat in Dad's desk chair, clasped his hands behind his head, and leaned back.

Wow! He looks like Dad. "I'm looking forward to the study."

"World religions, eh? Just remember they can all be wrong, but they can't all be right."

"Why not?"

"Some say there's only one God. Others claim thousands exist. They can't both be right."

"I guess not."

"Some say God cannot be known. Others say he's known in all things."

"I get it." Dawn relaxed into the leather chair on the other side of the desk.

"Good. Just seek the truth, and you'll find it."

"Like you and Mom did. But you said all religions could be wrong. What makes you think Christianity is right?"

A huge grin brightened Zeke's face. "That's simple. Christianity isn't a religion. It's a relationship."

"Whatever. I guess I'll have to discover the answers for myself."

"It's the only way." Zeke leaned forward, resting his elbows on the desk. "How's life?"

"My used-to-be friends avoid me like I'm an alien that escaped from the science lab. My teachers' displays of concern sicken me. My counselor at school, as well as the one downtown who charges Dad the sum of our inheritance, forces me to talk about things I'd rather let fade like a bad dream. Other than that, life's great. How about you?"

"Me?" Zeke sat up straight and stretched. "I'm doing okay. My job's pretty hectic, but I like it. Great pay."

"Cool."

"It's interesting how things fall into place, don't you think?" Zeke said. "Like my job...and you deciding to sell Sundance turned out to be a good thing since Dad decided to sell the farm. Are you okay with that?"

Dawn shrugged. "I don't really have much choice, do I? But I agree with Dad. It'll be a fresh start for all of us. So many memories here."

"So you really are good with it and ready to move on?" Zeke stood and headed to the kitchen with Dawn at his heels.

"Yeah, I think I am. Besides, Dad said it might take a year or more to sell the house and find a place in town. By then, I'll definitely be ready."

"Do you think you're up to a new adventure?"

"Like what?"

The kitchen door creaked as Dad entered.

"Dad?"

He smiled. "The last case was dismissed. Since we're all

home, let's go out for supper." He winked at Zeke, set his briefcase on the table, and walked back out the door.

Dawn furrowed her brows. "I think I'm being set up. What are you two conniving?"

"Just come on. I'm starved." Zeke held out his arm like a maître d'.

Dawn giggled and clasped his elbow as he ushered her to the back seat of the Jeep and helped her in, as though she needed the help. Anticipating the breezy ride in the topless vehicle, she twisted her hair into a knot.

Zeke jumped in behind the steering wheel, and with Dad on the seat next to him, sped down the road…past the local restaurant…through the small town of Farlee…finally turning into the drive to a place called The Kinetic Connections.

Dawn sat rigid and surveyed the grounds. "What are we doing here? I thought this was a camp for disabled kids. I didn't know they served meals here."

Tall pines bordered the groomed lawn on both sides of the lane. At the end of the driveway, a huge white-brick mansion nestled in the middle of a grove of blue spruce. The pine scent lingered on the crisp autumn air. Dawn wondered what lay beyond the thick tree line. She even thought she had heard a horse whinny in the distance.

"They do a lot of cool things here." Zeke parked in a reserved-for-guests stall, and the three walked into the main lobby. A mural of children enjoying playground equipment, playing ball, and riding horses clued Dawn in on the cool things Zeke had referred to. Maybe it was a horse whinnying. But why did they bring me here?

A short man with a receding hairline entered the room accompanied by an extremely thin, pale, African-American girl about Dawn's age. She sported an orange, turquoise, and brown paisley do-rag to cover her lack of hair, Dawn assumed.

The man shook Dad's and Zeke's hands vigorously. "Good seeing you again, Doug...Zeke."

"Good seeing you again too, Tim." Dad and Zeke said simultaneously as Dad placed his arm around Dawn's shoulder. "This is my daughter Dawn. Dawn, this is Tim Nephtalski."

Mr. Nephtalski extended an enthusiastic handshake to her as well. "It's good to finally meet you. Everyone around here calls me Mr. Neph."

He motioned to the girl. "This is Kimberly, one of our volunteers. I've asked her to show you round, Dawn, while your dad, brother, and I discuss some business. We'll join you at the stables in a few minutes."

Kimberly's dark eyes and cheerful smile brightened her ashen face. "Come on, Dawn." She wrapped a frail hand around Dawn's forearm and hurried to the door. "I'll show you the inside later, but let's explore the grounds first. I love the outdoors. How about you?"

"Yeah. I used to spend a lot of time outside." Dawn practically ran to keep up. *How can someone who looks so ill seem so happy…and move so fast?*

"Your hair is beautiful." Kimberly touched her do-rag. "I hope mine grows back nice and thick like yours. I'm actually starting to sprout."

Dawn nodded as she searched for the right words to say but found none.

"Hey, Hope." Two younger girls called from the playground.

"Hey, girls!" Kimberly waved then spoke to Dawn. "They call me Hope around here. See, I have this inoperable brain tumor and had to go through a long series of chemo treatments to shrink it. Time will tell how successful they were. I'm just glad to feel so good now. You can call me Hope too, if you'd like."

"I would." Dawn smiled. "You deserve the name."

"I'm told you know a lot about horses." Exhilaration rose in Hope's words, igniting an unexpected excitement in Dawn's heart.

Dawn shrugged. "I started riding lessons when I was five. I owned a horse for about six months, but I had to sell him."

"I'm around the horses a lot here and adore them all. I can't imagine selling a horse. Not that I ever owned one. That must've been devastating."

"About as devastating as...maybe a brain tumor?" *I shouldn't have said that. Nothing could be as devastating as a brain tumor, except maybe losing your mother and selling your beloved horse in the same month.*

"Yeah." Hope said solemnly. "I guess we have two things in common. We've both know life hurts and...." Her cheerful voice returned. "...and we both love horses."

"Cool, we both love horses...so we're a good match."

Hope slowed the pace as they approached the stables. "I

come here as often as I can. Being around the horses and helping children with disabilities helps me to cope with my illness. Come on, I'll show you our horses." She opened the door, and they walked in together.

"Great!" Dawn said. The sweet smell of horses and newly-mown hay flooded her mind with memories. Good memories. Memories Dawn wasn't prepared to face. She wiped away a tear with the back of her hand, refusing to allow any more to escape in front of Hope. *I didn't realize how much I miss Sundance...and Mom until now.*

"Our last stable girl left for college." Hope said. "We're looking for someone to replace her."

"So that's why Dad and Zeke brought me here."

"You didn't know?"

"I thought we were going out for supper."

"You are." Hope clapped her hands and giggled in pure delight as she revealed the surprise. "We...the kids...have prepared a special meal for you. A bribe of sorts. Please consider volunteering."

"Volunteering? As the stable girl?" *Oh, to be around horses again.* The thought fanned the spark of excitement already burning in Dawn's heart, which she attempted to ignore. "I don't think so. I mean...I don't have time with school projects and all."

Hope sighed. "Of course...what were we thinking? You're probably in all the school activities and busy with friends, cheerleading, and social events."

"No, not really." Dawn surveyed the stables. "Where are the horses?"

Hope's gaze swept the long hall of stalls. "They must all be outside. About volunteering...so, you're too busy with school?"

"I used to...but... not this year."

"So then you'll consider it?"

Dawn shrugged. "I don't know...."

A horse whinnied outside, a sound that cut to her heart. Dawn smiled. "Yeah, I'll consider it."

"Cool!" Hope handed Dawn a sugar cube. "Then let's go meet the horses. Wait until you see our newest arrival. If he doesn't convince you to volunteer nobody can." She pressed a finger to her lips and whispered, "Don't tell the others, but he's my favorite even though he seems depressed."

They walked outside and stood on the fence gate. Dawn admired the dozen or so horses grazing at the far end of the pasture. Hope whistled then clicked her tongue. "Here, Sundance!"

"Sundance?"

"Great name, huh? And it so fits him. His coat is a shimmering gold color like the sunset."

"Sundance?"

"Yeah, he's a gorgeous Palomino that arrived here about a month and a half ago with another beauty, a black Quarter Horse named Charlie."

The rumble of hoofs drew Dawn's attention to the horses trotting toward the fence. A familiar whinny filled the air as one horse broke into a full gallop until he reached the gate.

"That's my Sundance!" Dawn squealed. With tears streaming down her face, she climbed over the gate and threw her arms around her beloved horse's neck. In return he nickered and nudged her. "How did he get here?"

"Your Sundance?" Hope laughed and clapped again. "I don't know what made you get rid of him, but the two of you belong together. Anyone can see that."

Dawn stroked Sundance's neck and kissed his nose. "I don't believe this. Wait until Dad and Zeke see him!"

"So you've found Sundance." Mr. Neph strolled up to the fence and joined in the celebration with Dad and Zeke on his heels...their faces full of grins.

"Dad! Zeke! Look! It's my Sundance! Can you believe it? I thought you sold him at the auction?"

For the first time in months, Dad's eyes lit up with joy. "That was my plan, honey. But Zeke convinced me to donate both horses to this facility with the hopes of reuniting you and Sundance as soon as we felt you were ready." Suddenly, a look of deep concern washed over his face. "We were right in bringing you here today, weren't we?"

"Yeah, you were, Dad." Dawn glanced at Hope then back at Dad. *If this place can help her cope with a brain tumor, maybe it can help me cope with Mom's death.* "It feels good and right to be with Sundance again. New surroundings and a fresh start, kinda like us moving to a new house, right?"

As though he understood every word, Sundance shook his head and nickered.

Hope reached over the gate and stroked the horse's nose. "I hate to break up this awesome reunion, Dawn, but it's time to meet some of the greatest kids on earth."

"I'm looking forward to meeting them...and...I think I

really would like to help out here."

After giving Sundance another hug, Dawn crawled through the rails to join the others. As she and Hope walked back to the lodge arm-in-arm, Dawn glanced over her shoulder to admire her horse one more time. Joy, sorrow, anticipation, doubts, and fear all whirled within her, forming a new revelation.

There were no pat answers, no miracle cures, too few happy endings...but hope always remained. And maybe Hope...and Sundance were enough for now.

Ebony's Final Days

Lisa Krakovitz

"Mom, come here and look at this really neat horse!" Fifteen-year-old Patti Dornsife cautiously touched the white blaze of a coal black gelding in a stall at Butch's Livestock Auction. Ears pricked and eyes alert, the horse nodded and nickered. Patti stroked his velvety speckled nose, a gesture Patti was certain meant "Please bid on me and take me home." She raked her fingers through her long, wavy brown hair then petted the horse's sleek neck, taking note that, although he had a well-shaped head, his ribs were showing, and he had numerous cuts and scars all over his body. But to Patti, he was the most beautiful horse she had ever seen. She fell in love with him the moment she laid eyes on him.

An unusually warm Saturday in April had brought dozens of horse buyers and sellers to the central Pennsylvania sale held once a month. The large parking lot hosted dozens of cars, trucks, and Amish buggies, their owners congregating in the large red barn. There they registered and picked up a bidding number, bought hot dogs, fries, and whoopie pies from the snack counter, and sauntered through the holding pens to take a peek at the menagerie of horses and dairy cows that would be auctioned all afternoon.

"Mother, will you please come here!" Patti called past the mingling crowd to her mother. Ada Dornsife stood several yards away petting a large Shire work horse. "Mom, you gotta see this beautiful horse."

"I'm comin', I'm comin'!" Ada said. "Just hold your horses!" She weaved around a steady shuffle of onlookers and stood next to her daughter. "Well, he sure has a beautiful face, but he's so skinny. I can see his ribs."

"I want him, Mom," Patti said. "He's...he's just what I've always wanted." She petted the horse's neck, strengthening the bond already forming between the two.

"But he's so skinny, Patti. He might be sick."

"Not worth more than a couple hundred dollars," an Amish man said who stood looking at the horse. The man stroked his fuzzy, white beard then pointed at a flyer stapled to the pen. "Says here he's a registered paint Quarter Horse. Can't see how. There's not a bit of white on him 'cept that big wide blaze and two socks. And he could use another fifty pounds or so on him. Nah, no good for a driving horse." The man shook his head and walked away. "He'll probably go to the slaughterhouse."

Patti stared at the flyer and read the horse's name: Ebony. She glanced back at the horse, and her eyes filled with tears. *The slaughterhouse? He'll go for dog food?* "Mom, do you think that's true?"

Ada reached over the stall partition and petted the horse. "I don't know, Patti. I don't know beans about horses."

"We have to bid on him, Mom." She pointed at the flyer. "It says he's broke, so I'll be able to ride him. I didn't see another horse here that I liked. I want this one, Mom. Pl-lease."

Ada just stared at the horse.

"Mom, Elaine and her parents said we could keep a horse at their farm, didn't they?"

"Yeah, they did."

And Elaine and her sisters can ride him too, can't they? They're real good riders since they already have their own horses for years."

"Yeah, they can."

"Well?"

Ada gave her daughter a big smile. "I guess we'll bid on him. I know you've wanted a horse for a long time. Maybe now's the right time."

Eyes pooled with tears, Patti threw her arms around her mother's neck. "Oh thanks, Mom. You're the greatest."

Ada raised her index finger. "Now don't be too happy yet. Other people might bid on him, and I can only go so high. I don't own a gold mine, you know."

"We'll have to just pray—"

"You know, that's a good idea. Let's pray and ask the Lord if this is the horse for you."

*****

"Going once! Going twice! Sold! The three-year-old chestnut Shire goes for $800 to number 107, to the gentleman with the red hat in the gallery!" the auctioneer blurted through the loud speaker and pointed his gavel at a man in the fifth row.

Patti and Ada leaned against the fence on the center floor of the barn at auction. The surrounding gallery was packed with bidders, and although the spring weather was crisp and breezy, a strong pungent odor of manure hung in the air like a fog.

"The next horse is a registered four-year-old Pinto gelding, Ebony, green broke," the auctioneer blasted. "Good for trail riding. Bidding starts at $200."

The gate swung open and a husky man wearing a western outfit led in a fiery black horse that pranced like he was vying to pull the carriage for some foreign king.

"Oh, Mom," Patti said, "isn't he pretty?"

"Yeah, he is," Mom said. "But he looks like he's got a lot of spunk to him even though he's so skinny. Are you sure you can handle him?"

"Elaine and Bonnie will help me. And their dad is really good with horses too. I'll learn fast."

"Well, all right. We'll bid on him."

"Who'll start the bidding at $200?" the auctioneer asked.

And up went Ada's hand.

Four hundred dollars later, Ebony had a new home at Elaine and Bonnie Trevors' place, just a few miles down the road from Patti's house. Every chance Patti had, she went to her friends' farm to work with "her own horse." She brushed his coat until it almost sparkled, and she learned how to clean the hooves to ward off thrush, a nasty infection horses can get from standing in manure. But what to do about the horse's skinny condition? Patti also noticed that Ebony had a steady, nagging cough.

Dave, Bonnie's dad, looked the horse over and said, "Neither his thin body nor the cough is normal." With the man's vast horse know-how, he gave Patti and Ada a few tips to help the gelding gain weight and get rid of the cough.

"Depending on how much he's out to pasture, he should have at least a pound-size coffee can of oats or sweet feed twice a day and at least a section of alfalfa hay once or twice a day." Dave's dark brown eyes, framed in a green baseball cap, silver hair, and tan face, studied the horse. "We should worm him in case that's the reason he's so skinny. Worms will keep a horse's weight down, no matter how much you feed him. And worms can kill a horse."

"But if he doesn't have worms, he'll gain weight?" Patti asked.

"It'll take a few months, but we'll see a difference. And we'll give him some antibiotics for that cough. Hopefully, it's just a bit of a cold. But that could turn into pneumonia, so we have to be careful and keep an eye on that too."

Patti started following Dave's instructions to the T. As far as riding Ebony, she was ready the day after he arrived at the farm. But…there was only one problem….

"Ebony, will you keep still!" Elaine tried her best to slip the bit into the horse's mouth while Patti struggled to hold the horse's head steady. Every time Elaine made the attempt, Ebony pulled his head away, refusing to take the bit. Although the girls saddled him with no problem, the horse balked at the bridle…until Dave stepped in. Ebony still fought and pulled away, but Dave's experience and skill managed to slip on the bit.

"You better let me ride him first, girls," Dave said, "just to see if he has any quirks or bad habits. We don't want you to get hurt."

Dave mounted Ebony with no problem and for fifteen minutes rode him around the barn, through the fields, and on the township road that passed the farm. The horse responded well to neck reining, cantered smoothly, and seemed to have excellent trail manners.

"He's fine, Patti," Dave said, dismounting. He put the reins in Patti's hand. "I think it's time for you to try your horse."

"I'm really nervous," Patti said.

"You can't be nervous," Elaine said, her long straight brown hair framing brown eyes and a dimpled smile. "Horses can sense that. He might act up if you're shaking in your boots when you get on him."

"Boots?" Patti laughed and looked at her sneakers. "I don't even have boots yet."

"Just calm down," Dave said. "You've ridden our horses, so you'll be fine. Just walk him, pet his neck, and keep talking to him. But don't try to run him yet. Both of you need to get used to each other, and he needs to feel his way around the place. Just walk around the field and go up to the ridge and back."

"Okay," Patti said. She mounted her horse and carefully nudged Ebony's sides, following Dave's every instruction. In a few minutes, Elaine mounted her Quarter Horse mare and joined Patti in a nice half-hour walk around the farm.

Patti was all smiles through the entire ride. "He's really doing well, isn't he?" she asked Elaine, who rode alongside.

"Yep," she said. "He's doing great. You got yourself a really nice horse. A really nice horse."

*****

Over the next few months with a lot of TLC, Ebony put on the extra weight he needed, filling out nicely. He also lost the hacking cough and evolved into one handsome horse with a coat shinier than a black glass marble. Patti continued to care for him and ride regularly with her friends, always having a good, and safe, time.

However, as the summer progressed, Patti started noticing a difference in Ebony's demeanor. It seemed the more weight he gained, the more spirited…the more headstrong… he became. As a beginning rider, Patti became very cautious, almost fearful, of riding her horse because of the streak of stubbornness he started to display.

One beautiful September day, after Patti and Elaine tacked Ebony, still with a little fighting of the bit, Patti tried to mount. But the horse sidestepped and backed away, sending Patti's courage into a tailspin. Elaine, already mounted on her horse, waited.

"Ebony, what's the matter with you?" Patti stood beside him with a firm grip on the bridle.

Ebony neighed with his ears pricked, his neck arched, and his eyes full of devilment. No way was he going to allow Patti to climb on.

"Oh, for corn's sake," Elaine said, sliding off her horse. "Let me try. He's just feeling his oats."

The girls exchanged reins, and after several tries, Elaine mounted Ebony. "Just let me see how he's gonna behave," she said, turning him toward the field in back of the barn. "Wait here. I'll be back in a few minutes. C'mon, Ebony," she said, kicking him in the ribs.

"Be careful!" Patti yelled as Elaine started trotting Ebony past the barn and up a sloping field.

Patti stood with Elaine's horse, her gaze following every move Elaine and Ebony made. Up through the field they trotted then broke into a gallop...a fast gallop...back toward the barn. Elaine, her riding skills put to the test, tried her best to turn Ebony away from the barn. Suddenly with no warning, Ebony started to buck. Elaine yanked on the reins but lost her balance and flew off, hitting the ground hard while the horse tore back to the paddock next to the barn.

Patti stood frozen to the spot...shocked...as she watched Ebony, her beloved horse, pull such a stunt.

Completely unnerved, Patti tied Elaine's horse to a rail and ran to Elaine, who was struggling to stand. "Elaine, are you all right?"

"Yeah, nothing's broken as far as I can tell," she said, rubbing her elbow. "That's not the first time a horse threw me, but I sure didn't expect it out of Ebony. He's gone a little crazy!"

Nerves quivering and legs like Jell-o, Patti glanced at the paddock, where Ebony stood at the fence, his back leg cocked and his head drooped in leisure as if nothing unusual had happened for the last fifty years.

Elaine dusted herself off, and the girls headed back toward the barn.

"I just don't know what's wrong with him," Elaine said. "The only thing I can figure is that he's feeling too many of his oats now that he's got the extra weight on him. I guess he really is what we call green broke. He needs a lot of work."

"And I'm afraid I'm not the one to do it," Patti said, with tears in her eyes. "Elaine, I think my days of riding that horse are over."

*****

Patti, although she still dearly loved Ebony, had no desire to ever get on his back again. She brushed him and cared for him but never regained enough courage to even sit on him. With the passing of autumn, the horse's obnoxious behavior continued. He loved to run full speed in the pasture, to buck, and to kick his heels high in the air; yet, being ridden was what everyone knew he needed. But who would—could—ride the ornery fella?

Dave could control him and ride him, but Dave had no time to work with the horse.

How about rough-and-tough Jordan? One Saturday at a family gathering, Jordan, Elaine's brother-in-law, tried his hand at Ebony, but the horse had the upper hoof, dumping Jordan in the pasture just as he had done with Elaine.

Then there was the time the youth pastor from church said he'd try riding the horse, only to have Ebony stop abruptly when going down a small incline, lower his head, and launch the youth pastor into a heap on the ground.

By the spring of the following year, Patti and her mother had to make a tough decision, one of the toughest in Patti's life.

"Patti, we have to sell the horse. It's costing too much just to keep him without anyone being able to ride him."

"I know," Patti said. "I love him so much, but I'll be happy if we can find him a nice home with people who know how to train him and love him the way I do."

"We'll advertise him on the Internet," Ada said. "Maybe we'll get a good price in the sale and a good home for Ebony.

Several weeks passed with no offers from anyone. Finally in June, a young couple contacted Ada and Patti, wanting to see Ebony. Arrangements were made for Bill and Sue to stop by Trevors' farm the next Saturday.

"Oh, I just love him," Sue said, her blue eyes framed in long, blonde hair. "We're just new to the area, and we're in the process of buying a farm. He'll be my horse."

"We have to be honest with you," Ada said. "He needs a lot of work. He's only green broke, and he's bucked off a few people. My daughter's just learning to ride, and she's afraid to get on him since he threw some folks. That's why we decided to sell him. We're asking $800 for him."

"We just want him to have a good home," Patti said,

petting Ebony's neck.

Bill squared his Stetson on his short, dark hair, his smile tentative. "Oh, he'll have a good home. We want to board horses at our place for a few extra bucks. On the side, I'll work with Ebony and make him a safe ride for even a kid."

"All we ask is that he gets a good home," Ada said.

"He will with us," Sue said. "He'll have a forever home with us, and you can come see him anytime. All you need to do is call."

*****

A week after Bill and Sue picked up Ebony, Patti called their number. She missed her horse so much, she wanted to go visit him. But Bill and Sue never returned her call. In fact, they never returned numerous calls over the next few weeks. Worried about Ebony's fate, Patti went online to a few horse sales sites and found Ebony for sale on one of the sites for $3500!

Patti and Ada were terribly distraught, feeling they had been deceived and taken. Hoping Ebony would be sold to a good home, Patti watched the sales site over the next few weeks, noticing Ebony's price drop quickly to $800. She continued to call the number Bill had given her, and finally he returned her call in mid-August.

"Why are you selling Ebony?" Patti asked with a twinge of disgust. "You told us you were going to keep him forever."

"Our plans changed over the last few months," Bill said. "We're moving again, and we have to sell him. Do you want him back?"

"We can't take him back," Patti said.

"Well then, we'll sell him to someone else. Our business with you has ended. Goodbye."

*****

"Butch's Livestock Auction is this Saturday, Mom," Patti said. "I wonder if those people will try to sell Ebony there."

"There's only one way to find out," Ada said. "We'll go and check it out."

Sure enough, on Saturday when Patti and Ada made their rounds in the auction barn, they found Ebony, a little thinner but in pretty good shape.

"Mom, I wanna stay and see who buys him." Patti stroked Ebony's nose, and he responded with an I-know-you nicker. "Maybe they'll let us visit him at his new home."

"I'm sure some nice folks will buy him," Ada said. "He's

too pretty to go to the slaughterhouse. We'll stay and see what happens to him."

An hour later Patti and Ada sat in the gallery, watching the bids on Ebony as he pranced around the holding pen. Chewing her nails, Patti let her nerves get the best of her, wondering where her beloved horse would go next. Finally, the bidding closed.

"Sold to Reich's Livestock for $450!" the auctioneer blared over the loud speaker. "You got yourself a nice-looking gelding there."

"I hope that livestock place will find a good home for him," Patti said, a shot of worry coursing through her veins.

Ada relaxed in her seat and let out a sigh of relief. "Patti, I think he's going to a good place. All the poor horses that are going for slaughter are old or lame, and they went for $50 or $100."

"Let's go see Ebony one last time," Patti said, tears flooding. "One last time."

*****

The next day, just for curiosity's sake, Ada decided to investigate Reich's Livestock and discovered the owner was a broker, who bought and sold horses for profit, but he also was a "kill buyer," who shipped horses to Canada for slaughter. Horrified at the thought of Ebony becoming dog meat, Ada searched the Internet for horse rescue ranches and found the Lifeline Horse Rescue near Allentown, Pennsylvania, an agency that had rescued other horses from Reich's Livestock. She immediately called the number.

"Hello, Lifeline Horse Rescue," the female voice said. "Bailey speaking."

"Bailey, this is Ada Dornsife from central Pennsylvania. My daughter and I are concerned about a horse we sold, and through some misdealings, somehow, has landed at Reich's Livestock. Do you have any way of finding out if Ebony will be placed in a good home or sold for slaughter? I'm terribly upset over this whole situation. And I haven't been able to tell Patti that her horse might be killed."

"Give me a little more information and your phone number," Bailey said. "I'll have an answer for you in an hour or so."

True to her word, Bailey called back in a little while. "Ada, I have bad news. Reich is sending Ebony to a slaughterhouse in Canada—tomorrow."

Ada's throat tightened, and her eyes flooded with tears.

"We can't let that happen. We just can't. My daughter's heart will be broken. What can we do to save him?"

"I wish I could take him," Bailey said, "but I'm filled to the gills here with rescued animals. I'll give you the number of Miranda, a friend of mine who also has another rescue in our area, the Hope for Horses Rescue Ranch. I think she has room, so I know she can help you."

Ada called Miranda, who was more than willing to help. "I've dealt with Reich before, and I'll give him a call. He'll probably want a few hundred more than he paid for the horse. Send me all Ebony's information and a picture of him."

"Please hurry," Ada said. "He's shipping Ebony out tomorrow."

A while later, Miranda texted Ada. Reich wants $650 for Ebony.

Ada texted back. I don't have that kind of money. What can we do?

I'll raise the money online. Check my page on Facebook in a few hours.

At eight-thirty the same evening, Ada logged onto Facebook. When she found the Hope for Horses site, she was overwhelmed with what she saw.

The picture of Ebony and Patti, which Ada had sent to Miranda, had been posted with a plea to all horse lovers to save Ebony's life by making a contribution. Over sixty donations had been made, paying all but $190 to buy Ebony from Reich. Shortly after viewing the site, Ada received a call from Miranda, asking if Ada could finance the rest.

"I live on a tight budget and a very limited income," Ada said, "but I'll give the rest. I just have to, for Ebony's sake…and for Patti's."

"If you can pay that last amount for Reich, we have enough funds here to pay for transportation costs and shots."

"Shots?" Ada asked.

"Ada," Miranda said, "I don't have room for Ebony here, but I know of a rescue ranch in New England. The owners will gladly take Ebony and will let him live out his days there. You need never fear for his life again."

Tears trickled down Ada's face as she thanked Miranda for her generosity and kind deed. Just when Ada clicked off her phone, Patti came into the living room.

"Mom, what's the matter? Is Ebony okay? Why are you

crying?"

"Patti, I didn't want to tell you about Ebony until I knew everything was okay with him. Reich planned to ship Ebony to a slaughterhouse in Canada—tomorrow."

Patti burst into tears. "Oh, Mom—"

"Now hold on." Ada gave her daughter a big smile and a bigger hug. "There's a rescue ranch near Allentown that just raised almost all the money needed to buy Ebony from Reich. I threw in the last $190."

Patti wiped her wet cheeks, a quizzical look draping her face as she stared into her mother's eyes. "Ebony's safe? Where is he?"

"He's at Reich's, but he's being transported to the Hope for Horses Rescue Ranch near Allentown as soon as possible."

"But, Mom, where'd you get $190? We don't have extra money like that."

"I robbed Peter to pay Paul, but that's okay. With a little belt tightening, our bills will all be paid at the end of next month. What's important is that Ebony's safe. God answered a lot of prayers over the last twenty-four hours. This time Ebony is going to a forever home."

"Where? Will we be able to visit him?"

"He's going to a rescue ranch in Maine. As far as visiting him, it will have to be by pictures only."

"I still miss him so much, but I'm so glad he's going to a safe place, even if it is so far away."

R-R-Ring. Ada's cell phone rang. She clicked on the phone and glanced at the wall clock. Ten o'clock.

"Hello."

"Ada, this is Miranda. I want you to know that we just picked up Ebony. He's here at our ranch, and in a week or so, we'll move him to his forever home up north."

"Thank you so much," Ada said. "I can't thank you enough. God bless you."

*****

The next Saturday, Ada, Elaine, and Patti traveled to a shopping mall near Allentown. So Patti thought.

"Mom, where are we going?" Patti examined the farmlands as they sped down the highway. "We already drove past Allentown."

"You'll see in a little while," Ada said.

In ten minutes, the car pulled into a driveway leading to a farm about a hundred yards away. At the roadside, a sign informed all visitors of the place that had become so special to Patti and Ada Dornsife.

"Hope for Horses Rescue Ranch!" Patti almost burst with excitement.

"Is this the place that rescued Ebony?" Elaine asked.

"Yep," Ada said. "I want you to meet Miranda. She did all the calling, posting on Facebook, and fundraising. We owe her big time. I want to thank her personally."

"When did they send Ebony to Maine?" Patti asked as the car pulled in front of the barn. A husky woman with short red hair and a smile from ear to ear met them.

"That must be Miranda," Ada said, turning the car off. "C'mon, girls."

The three got out of the car and joined the woman.

"You must be Ada," the woman said. "I'm Miranda."

Ada smiled and pointed to her companions. "Yes, and this is my daughter, Patti, and her friend, Elaine."

Miranda extended her hand to all three. "I'm so glad to meet you all. People like you are so important to the work we do to rescue animals. We couldn't do it without your support."

"When did Ebony get shipped to New England?" Patti

asked. "I just need to know that he's safe from now on."

"Say," Miranda said, "would you gals like a tour of our place? How would you like to see all our rescued horses?"

"Sure," Elaine said. "I love horses of any size and shape, especially happy ones."

Patti pointed at Elaine and smiled. "She lives on a farm too, and they have two horses. That's where we kept Ebony when I owned him."

Miranda turned toward the barn door and gestured for the three to follow. "C'mon. I'll show you the latest horses we rescued."

The four walked in and strolled down a short hallway to a row of open stalls on the left side of the barn. All except one were empty with their resident horses grazing outside.

There three stalls down, standing with his neck arched, his ears pointed, and his speckled nose flaring was—

"Ebony!" Patti and Elaine said at the same time.

Patti ran to the stall and threw her arms around the horse. As usual, he gave her a welcoming nicker. "He's still here! Oh, Ebony!"

Elaine and Ada hurried to the stall and petted the horse.

"Patti, I wanted you to see him one last time before he

goes to his new home," Ada said. "Miranda was nice enough to say yes, so here we are."

"Mom, you're the greatest," Patti said.

"Ebony looks real good, doesn't he?" Elaine said.

"He's been eating me out of house and home," Miranda joked. "From now on, he has a life of leisure. And once Ebony gets to his forever home, Chuck will send me pictures, and I'll send them to you."

"Thank you so much," Ada said to Miranda. "This is such a special treat for us."

"I thought we were going to a mall," Patti said. "But this is the best surprise I've ever had in my entire life."

Elaine rubbed Ebony's nose. "And what do you think of that, fella?"

Ebony nickered then nodded to let Patti know he agreed with every word that had just been said.

Sadie and the Princess

Beth Westcott

More than anything in the world, Sadie Rose Collins wanted a horse of her own. She read horse stories, and she hung horse posters all around her bedroom. She dreamed of riding her horse and winning blue ribbons in horse shows. She had ridden ponies at the fair and the mall, but that was just in circles, around and around. And the rides always ended too soon.

"We can't afford a big animal like a horse," Kevin, her father, had explained even before they moved. "Horses cost a lot of money to buy. Then you have to pay for hay and grain and veterinary care. It's too expensive for us. Besides, we don't have a place to keep a horse. Maybe someday."

"I know how you feel, Sadie," said her mother. "I wanted a horse too, and I had to be satisfied riding a friend's horse occasionally. It won't hurt to pray. Talk to God about how you feel."

Her little brother tugged on her hand. "I'll pray too." Four-year-old Nathan didn't like to be left out of family conversations.

Sadie glanced at Nathan. "What if God says no?" she asked her parents.

Slipping his arm around his daughter's shoulders, Dad said, "I know how much you want a horse, but you can't always have what you want. I've learned that God's way is best, even when I think my own idea is better."

Sadie sighed and nodded. *I knew better than to argue.*

The Collins family had moved into their new home at the beginning of last summer. Even though it had been hard to leave her former home, friends, and school, Sadie loved the big, two-story house with a large front porch and yellow siding. Sugar maple trees bordered the wide back yard, leaving plenty of space for the newly-planted garden and a play area for her and Nathan.

Whenever she arrived home from school, the pet golden retriever, Kip, greeted her in the driveway with glad barks and a wagging tail. Smokey the cat jumped down from the porch swing, stretched, and rubbed against the girl's leg. Sadie sat on the porch steps to pet the dog and cuddle the purring cat. She loved the family pets dearly, but she still wished for a beautiful horse of her own.

But as usual, Sadie played catch with Kip and cuddled Smokey, all the while praying she could have a horse, yet doubting that God would bother answering her prayer because He had so many more important things to do.

As the spring days became warmer, Sadie rode her bike to and from school because the Collins' home bordered the edge of town. Farm land dotted the countryside. Around the corner where she turned from Main Street onto Sassafras Lane toward home, she passed a curving driveway that led up a knoll to a white house with green trim. A red stable enclosed by a rail fence stood a short distance from the house. Sadie sometimes saw a car parked beside the house, but she never saw the people who lived there.

One day, after the grass turned green and began to grow, she noticed a horse grazing in the pasture. She skidded her bike to a stop and gazed at the horse with its shaggy gray hair and tangled black mane and tail. The stable door stood open behind the horse.

"If you were my horse," Sadie whispered, "I'd brush you until you'd sparkle, and I'd ride you every day."

After a few minutes, she sighed. "Bye," she said as she pedaled away toward home.

Every day for the next two weeks, Sadie stopped her bike at the side of the road to look at the horse. More than ever she wanted her own horse, and the gray horse filled her dreams.

One day, when Sadie stopped near the pasture fence, the gray horse looked at her and whinnied. The horse took a few steps toward the fence, her ears pricked, her neck arched. Sadie laid her bike on the ground and pulled out a handful of lush, green grass and clover from along the roadside. She straightened and shifted her backpack back into place. Holding the grass near the horse, Sadie spoke softly. "Here, girl."

The horse limped to the fence and sniffed at Sadie. She had a white diamond on her forehead and four black socks on her legs. She cautiously took a nibble of grass from the girl's hand. Sadie slowly reached out to touch the horse.

"Hey! What are you doing to my horse?" a man shouted from the driveway beside the pasture.

The horse jerked her head back at the loud, angry sound, and Sadie jumped back, dropping the rest of the grass. She hadn't noticed the car parked next to the house or that the man had come outside.

Trembling, Sadie turned to the man, whose face reflected agitation. "N-nothing," she said. "J-just giving her s-some grass." Sadie steadied her bike and climbed on.

"You have no business bothering my horse. I'll—"

"I'm s-sorry. The horse looked hungry and came to the fence. I th-think she has a sore foot."

"I know how to take care of a horse. Go home! Don't meddle where you're not wanted!"

Sadie raced home as fast as her legs could peddle. Tears blinding her eyes, she nearly rode into a ditch beside the road. At home she parked her bike in the garage and ran in the back door, ignoring the welcome of the family pets.

"I'm home, Mom!" she called with a quivering voice as she ran upstairs, refusing her usual cookies and milk in the kitchen. She also ignored Nathan when he said, "Sadie, look at...." Slamming her door and throwing her book bag on the bed, she flopped in her chair at her desk and stared out the window, the tears in her eyes blurring her view.

Minutes later she heard a quiet knock at her door. Sadie wiped the tears from her face and took her math book from her book bag. "Come in," she said.

Sadie's mother opened the door and peeked in. "You didn't get your cookies and milk." She came into the room. "Nathan has been waiting all day to show you something he made. Is everything okay?" She set a small plate with two cookies and a glass of milk on the desk. Gently she stroked Sadie's long, brown hair.

The girl shook her head and sniffed. "No, not really."

"Do you want to talk about it?"

Sadie did, but she was afraid she'd start crying again. The man's angry voice had frightened her. And just maybe she had been wrong to touch the horse without permission from the owner. "Not right now. I have to do my homework."

"Maybe later then. I'll be in the kitchen getting dinner."

"Okay, Mom. Thanks."

"I love you," said Sadie's mother as she closed the door.

An hour later, after Sadie finished her homework, she went downstairs to set the table for dinner. She smiled when Nate proudly showed her his "project." "Good job," she said as she admired the ship model he had built with his blocks earlier that day.

During dinner she knew her parents waited for her to talk to them about her problem. But knowing how they felt about her having her own horse, she hesitated to tell them about the gray horse. Besides, she didn't want to be accused of picking a fight with them.

She talked a little about school, and Nathan chattered about his day. She listened intently as her father read the Bible and prayed during family devotions. She even dried the dishes, practiced her piano lesson without complaining, and played with Nathan until his bedtime.

She gave Mom and Dad extra big hugs before going up to bed. "Good night," she said.

"You've been quiet tonight, Sadie. Is everything okay?" asked her father as he returned her hug.

She shrugged. "Just thinking," she said. She hesitated at the bottom of the stairs and glanced at them, shook her head, then climbed the stairs to her room. As she got ready for bed, she had a special prayer to God. "Please, dear Lord, show me a way to help that horse. Tomorrow I'll talk to Sasha. Maybe she can help."

Sadie's best friend, Sasha Jacobs, was a year older than Sadie. Their families went to the same church and spent time together. Sasha attended middle school next to the elementary school where Sadie attended fifth grade. The girls tried to meet for a few minutes before and after school every day on the sidewalk between the two buildings.

Sasha readjusted the rubber band on her long black ponytail and listened as Sadie told her about the shaggy gray horse and the angry man. "I want to help that horse, Sasha. I don't think that man treats her very well." Sadie's eyes pooled with tears. "We're supposed to respect adults, but how can we when they do bad things?"

"I know," Sasha said. "Do you remember my Aunt Amiya?"

Sadie nodded. "Yeah, I do. What about her?"

Sasha continued. "She rescued some of the horses she has now from owners who didn't take care of them. I'm sure she can help."

"Oh, Sasha, do you think so? Thank you! Thank you!"

Sadie threw her arms around her friend, and they hugged.

Sasha laughed. "I haven't done anything yet. But you're welcome anyway. What are friends for?" Sasha turned and headed toward the middle school building. "See ya!"

"See you later!" Sadie headed into her school, feeling much better after telling Sasha. *Maybe God does have time to listen to my prayers.*

*****

That afternoon, the gray horse looked up and whinnied as Sadie rode past.

"Help is on the way," Sadie whispered, but she never stopped. The angry man had made it perfectly clear he didn't want her around the horse.

"Did you know that Sasha's aunt rescues horses from bad owners?" she asked her parents at the dinner table that evening.

Dad raised his eyebrows when he looked at Sadie. "Amiya Jacobs is quite a horsewoman. She trains horses and has won many ribbons in horse shows."

Sadie only knew that Sasha's aunt owned horses. After a long pause, she asked, "Have you seen the shaggy gray horse in the pasture down the road?"

Mom laid down her fork. "Are you thinking about rescuing that horse?"

Sadie's eyes filled with tears. "I don't think the man loves her, Mom. She needs to be brushed, and she has a sore foot."

"That's not good, is it, Dad?" asked Nathan, waving his spoon in the air.

"No, it's not," Father answered. "But I've seen the horse, and I know something about the man, Carl Gleeman. Don't judge him before you know the facts, Sadie Rose."

"But, Daddy, the horse needs help. She needs someone who'll love her and take care of her."

"You know we can't afford a horse for you, Sadie," said her mother.

"But can't I try to help her?" The girl stared earnestly at her mother and father.

Dad laid his hand on his daughter's arm. "God wants us to take care of animals, but we can't just go in there and take the man's horse away from him. I'll tell you what—let me talk to Sasha's aunt. Then we'll decide what to do. We want to handle this in the right way. Are you willing to wait?"

Sadie sighed and nodded. "Okay, Dad, I'll try to wait.

I'll ask God for a way to help that horse."

"Me too," said Nathan.

"Good!" Mom beamed a broad smile. "Remember to pray for Mr. Gleeman as well."

Sadie waited and waited. It seemed like forever, but only two days later on Saturday, an African-American woman driving a blue pick-up pulled into the Collins' driveway. Kip barked his head off, as usual, and the Collins family, all working in the yard in the warm spring morning, looked up.

"Dad, look! Is that Sasha's aunt Amiya?" Sadie asked.

Dad turned off the lawn mower as Sadie and her mother pulled off the gloves they wore while weeding the garden. Nathan stopped dropping stones from the garden into his small, plastic wagon. They all walked over to greet the young woman in the truck.

Wearing jeans, a blue plaid shirt, and boots, her hair in a French braid down her back, the woman jumped out of the truck and paused to pet the dog running to her with his wagging tail.

After greeting one another and commenting about the nice spring weather, Amiya smiled at Sadie. "Your dad and my niece told me you're worried about the gray horse down the road."

Sadie nodded. "Yes, I think she needs help."

"Why don't we all go sit down and discuss this problem." Dad pointed to the back porch.

They sat around a picnic table on the porch, Sadie on the same side as Amiya. Nathan crowded in beside his sister. Smokey, lying in a sunny spot on the porch, raised her head and gave them a sleepy blink, then put her head back down. Kip lay in the sunshine at the foot of the steps, moving only his eyes as he watched the people. Mom brought out bright pink glasses and a pitcher of lemonade then sat down next to her husband on the other side of the table.

Amiya cleared her throat. "Let me tell you something about the horse and the man who owns her," she said. She took a sip of lemonade. "I trained the gray horse. Her name is Princess Cassandra, and she's a show horse." She took a deep breath. "At least she was."

"Princess Cassandra—what a beautiful name!" said Sadie.

"Yes, she was a beautiful mare and a top show horse." Amiya released a cautious smile. "I also taught the girl who owned her how to ride. You should have seen them together. They won many ribbons. I think the girl was on her way to becoming a member of the Olympic equestrian team."

"What's the girl's name," Sadie asked.

"Elizabeth. Elizabeth Gleeman."

"Oh," exclaimed Sadie. "That's the man's last name! I haven't seen her around. Where is she now? Doesn't she still ride?"

Amiya rubbed her thumb across her glass and sighed. "Two summers ago Elizabeth and her mother were in a terrible car accident. Cynthia Gleeman got hurt, but Elizabeth was killed." Amiya's voice broke, and she bit her lip.

"Oh, my!" Mom said.

"How awful!" Sadie whispered.

Tears welled up in Mother's eyes as Sadie's parents clasped each other's hands. Nathan leaned his head against Sadie's arm, fully understanding the seriousness of the discussion.

Amiya continued, "Yes, it was. Carl took it very hard. His wife is mostly better now, but they both miss Elizabeth very much. Carl won't sell Princess Cassandra, although he doesn't spend much time with her. I volunteered to care for the horse at my place, but he won't let her go."

Sadie glanced at her father. "That's what you meant when you said not to judge before I knew the facts, isn't it, Dad?"

He nodded. "When a parent loses a child, it's a terrible thing."

"Carl loves that horse," Amiya said. "He's just been going through a difficult time. Princess Cassandra doesn't get the extra loving care that Elizabeth used to give her, but she gets enough to eat and has shelter. She's a healthy horse."

But why does she limp? Sadie's feelings churned inside, glad that Princess Cassandra was all right but sad because Elizabeth had died. Sadie glanced at her own parents, thinking how sad they would be if she or Nathan died.

Amiya broke the silence around the table that followed her story. "Sasha told me you want a horse, but your family can't afford one."

"Yes, that's true," Sadie said. "But I understand why I can't have one."

"Well, I have an idea that maybe everyone will go for. If you really want to help Princess Cassandra, and you are willing to work hard, there may be something you can do…if your parents agree." She looked at Mom and Dad.

Mom and Dad looked at each other then nodded. "We're listening," Dad said.

Amiya leaned on the table. "This is what we will do…."

*****

When Sadie and her dad jumped out of Amiya's truck later that day, the butterflies in her stomach fluttered all the way down to her toes. Amiya had called and arranged a meeting…a very special meeting…with Mr. Gleeman.

But Sadie's nerves had gotten the best of her, remembering the man's frowning face and angry words. Although she thought she never wanted to talk to Mr. Gleeman again, she changed her mind, willing to do almost anything to help the man's beautiful horse.

When Carl Gleeman came out of the barn, he greeted everyone…with a smile! He then reached out and shook Amiya's hand. "Amiya, it's good to see you again. It has been a while since…." He swallowed hard.

Why, he looks like a friendly person after all! Sadie thought.

"Hello, Carl," Amiya said. "It's good to see you too. How's your wife?"

"She's much better, although she still uses a cane. Thank you for asking." He glanced at Dad and Sadie then shifted back to Amiya. "How are the plans for the handicapped riding program coming along?"

Amiya smiled. "I hope to be opening next year." She looked at Sadie and Dad. "It's been my dream to open a riding school for physically and mentally-challenged kids. It looks like it will happen soon."

"Sounds like a good thing," said Dad.

Sadie had heard that people sometimes used animals, including horses, to help children who had physical or mental disabilities. She wanted to ask more about it, but Mr. Gleeman began talking again.

"Now, you wanted to talk about Cassandra?" he asked Amiya.

"Have you met the Collins family? They bought the Sanders' place last summer. This is Kevin Collins and his daughter, Sadie Rose."

The two men shook hands. When Mr. Gleeman took Sadie's hand, he said, "You're the girl on the bicycle who stopped to see Cassie."

The girl bit her lip. "Yes, sir."

"I'm sorry I yelled at you. I shouldn't have. It's just that...the horse...." He cleared his throat and looked at Princess Cassandra, who watched from the pasture, her ears pricked.

Sadie swallowed, trying to ease the lump in her throat. "That's all right, Mr. Gleeman," she said gently. "I'm sorry about your daughter. I wish I could have known her."

"Thank you." Mr. Gleeman touched her shoulder. "You're very kind."

"Sadie wants a horse, Carl," Amiya said, "but her family can't afford to keep one. I think she may be able to help you."

The man raised his eyebrows as he looked at Amiya, then at Sadie, whose heart raced like a Thoroughbred at the finish line. "Oh? How?"

"Sadie has agreed that, if you let her, she'll come to spend time with Cassandra. The horse could use some TLC."

Carl Gleeman sighed and shook his head. "Well, I can't deny that."

Amiya continued. "Sadie said she's willing to work hard

and even clean the stall every day. She doesn't want any pay. All she wants to do is care for Cassandra and ride her. I'll teach her…if you'll let us.

Carl hesitated. "I don't have a lot of spare time for Cassie. She looks rough."

"But that's the point, Mr. Gleeman," Amiya said. "We'll care for her."

"I'll be very careful and love her like she's mine," Sadie promised. "Oh, please, please say yes."

Mr. Gleeman looked at Dad. "And you agree to this?"

Dad nodded. "My wife and I feel this would be a great opportunity for our daughter. We know how much she wants a horse. We respect Amiya's opinion and skill. She has agreed to teach Sadie how to ride and how to take care of the horse. Hope and I think we can work out a schedule so Sadie will keep up with her schoolwork and other responsibilities. She will have plenty of time to spend with the horse."

Holding her breath, her heart thumping, Sadie watched every move Mr. Gleeman made. She waited for an answer…twisting a lock of hair around her fingers.

Finally Mr. Gleeman spoke, his face at first sober but

then breaking into a smile. "I think something can be worked out. Cassie misses Elizabeth so much…as we all do. Definitely she needs another girl."

"Oh, thank you, Mr. Gleeman." Sadie threw her arms around the man. "You won't be sorry."

For a moment the man stood staunch, stiff…but then wiped the corner of his eyes like he was flicking away a piece of dirt. Slowly his arm slipped around Sadie's shoulders. "No, I don't think I'll be sorry at all." He pointed toward the pasture. "Come on, let me introduce you to Princess Cassandra. Then I'll show you why she limped the other day and how I helped her. I had to remove a stone caught in her hoof."

As Mr. Gleeman led Sadie to the gate, Dad and Amiya leaned on the fence, watching. When Mr. Gleeman opened the gate, Princess Cassandra whinnied and trotted to them with no limp at all! Stopping in front of Mr. Gleeman, the mare stood with her neck arched, ears pricked, and a soft nicker as the man spoke. He slipped his arm around her neck and leaned his head against the horse's face.

Sadie cautiously walked toward them, holding her breath and reaching out her hand.

Almost as if she knew Sadie, Cassandra stretched her neck, sniffed Sadie's hand, then released a gentle snort, a "hello, how are you?" in horse language. Sadie giggled at the gentle tickle of the horse's breath and could hardly contain her excitement. "She is so beautiful!"

"That she is," Mr. Gleeman said. "And I can see she already likes you."

Mr. Gleeman pulled an apple from his pocket and handed it to Sadie. "Give this to her. Put it on your palm and hold your fingers out straight."

Sadie did as she was told and felt the soft tickle of the horse's lips as she took the apple.

"What do you think, Sadie?" Dad said with a chuckle from the sidelines. "Do you want to work with that horse or not?"

"Maybe she's changing her mind now that she's up close and personal." Amiya laughed.

"Are you kidding?" Sadie said. "This is a dream come true."

Mr. Gleeman continued to pet the horse. "She still has her winter coat. See how shaggy she is? But I have a feeling she'll be shining like a silver dollar in no time."

I have been so wrong about Mr. Gleeman, Sadie concluded. *It really isn't right to judge people without knowing the facts. And I bet he loves Cassandra more that I could ever imagine because Elizabeth had loved her so much. I'll make it up to him by caring for his horse the best way I know how.*

*****

Sadie worked hard all that spring and summer, taking care of Princess Cassandra and riding her whenever she had the chance. In just a few short days, the horse's coat did shine like a silver dollar from the currying Sadie did, and Amiya taught her how to braid the horse's mane and tail. Every day Sadie cleaned Cassie's hooves with a pick, checking for dirt and stones and anything else that might cause infection and lameness. Although Sadie struggled some days to get up at the crack of dawn, ride her bike to Gleemans, then feed Cassie, brush her and muck the stall…all before breakfast, she tried her best not to complain. But once in a while it slipped out at the table…followed by a reprimand from her father.

Dad looked at her over his coffee mug. "If you had your own horse, you would have even more responsibility. Mr. Gleeman and Princess Cassandra are depending on you.

You made a commitment to them."

Sadie sighed. "I know, Dad. And Amiya is a good teacher too. I'm sorry, but sometimes I get so tired. I'll try not to complain."

"That's my girl," Dad said with his usual broad smile.

Once school ended for summer vacation, Sadie found it easier to fulfill her responsibilities and care for the horse. Carl and Cynthia Gleeman became like Sadie's favorite aunt and uncle.

Sometimes Sasha came with her aunt to help Sadie with Cassie and watch the riding lessons.

One day Sadie asked her friend a question while they groomed the mare.

"Sasha, why don't you ride? Your aunt could teach you."

"Oh, I can ride. Aunt Amiya made sure of that. We'll have to go riding together some day at Aunt Amiya's."

"But I've never seen you ride."

Sasha shrugged. "I like horses, but I don't want to spend all my time caring for or showing. I ride strictly for fun. I like sports in school better, that's all."

Sasha had long legs and ran fast. Sadie had watched her

compete in several track meets. She had seen her friend play soccer and basketball. And although Sadie preferred horses, she and Sasha were still best friends.

"I don't mind playing in gym class or with my friends for fun," Sadie said. "I'm glad you know how to ride. I think it would be fun to ride together."

*****

Later in the summer, with only three weeks left before she entered middle school, Sadie proudly brushed Cassie in the paddock on Mr. Gleeman's farm. While Sadie babied the horse, Mr. and Mrs. Gleeman with Sadie's parents and brother prepared the back yard for a picnic, grilling hot dogs, setting supplies on a picnic table, and carrying a cooler of soda outside.

Sadie glanced at Mr. Gleeman and smiled, reflecting how her life…his life…his horse's life had changed. Four months ago a horse had been only a dream of Sadie's…a wild, distant dream she thought she'd never see. But now? Next week she and Princess Cassandra would be in their first horse show together.

The horse's dark gray coat lay smooth and shiny, like silver, her black mane and tail neatly braided. Cassie nudged

Sadie's shoulder with her head. In an equal gesture of affection, Sadie stroked the horse's soft muzzle. It seemed as though she had always known the beautiful horse, who had become her best friend...next to Sasha, of course.

A blue pick-up pulled into the driveway, and Sasha and her aunt jumped out, having been invited to the picnic. Both made a beeline to the paddock.

"Cassandra is so gorgeous," said Sasha, stroking the horse's sleek neck. "I think she'll be the most beautiful horse in the show."

Amiya smiled at her niece and rubbed the horse's muzzle. "Sadie, you've worked hard and have done so well. I think you're ready for the show."

"If you hadn't helped me, and Mr. Gleeman hadn't let me take care of Cassie, I wouldn't be in a horse show. And I wouldn't have all of you as friends."

"Sadie," Amiya said, her dark brown eyes sparkling with a mischievous twinkle, "now that you've learned so much about horses, I'm wondering if you'd be interested in another project." She shifted her glance to Sasha. "And you too, Sasha."

"I hope by next spring I'll have my special needs riding

academy open," Amiya said. "There are a lot of regulations I have to comply with, and the licensing process is long, but I have a goal in mind."

"Will you still train horses?" Sasha asked.

"At first I will. It'll depend on how many students I have."

Sadie said, "You mean you'll teach them to ride?"

"To ride and to help take care of the horses. And I'd like to use rescued horses, if I can. Some of them have sweet temperaments. I'm sure they'll help the kids."

"That sounds cool. I wish I could help," said Sadie.

"Me, too," Sasha agreed.

Sadie looked at her friend. "I thought you didn't want to spend a lot of time with horses."

"Well," said Sasha, "I think I'd like doing that."

"And that's the very project I'd like you'd to do. You can be my first two volunteers. I'm going to need lots of help."

"Time to eat!" called Carl Gleeman from the grill. "The hot dogs are ready."

"We're coming, Mr. G.!" Sadie finished brushing Cassandra and released her into the pasture. Joining Sasha and Amiya outside the fence, the three hurried toward the others who were gathering around the table, ready to enjoy the fruits of the Gleemans' labor.

As Sadie walked with her friends, she couldn't help send a prayer of thanks toward heaven for the way God had answered her prayer...and in such a miraculous way.

"Dear God," she prayed, "thank you for Cassandra. You answered my prayer for a horse, but in such a different way than I wanted. Thank you for Mr. and Mrs. Gleeman, and thank you for letting us spend time together. In Jesus' name, amen."

As Sadie approached the table, she glanced back at Princess Cassandra grazing in the field with her beautiful gray coat shining like a silver dollar.

God really did give me more than I could ever imagine, Sadie thought, and all she could do was smile.

We horse lovers hope you loved these heartwarming tales about our favorite animal. For more horse stories and horse books, check out www.marshahubler.com

www.ingramcontent.com/pod-product-compliance
Lightning Source LLC
Chambersburg PA
CBHW060054150626
46556CB00017BA/438